The Pigs Feet Murder

Martin Coffey

Best Wishes
Martin Coffey

Copyright © Martin Coffey, 2023
First Published in Ireland, in 2023, in co-operation with
Choice Publishing, Drogheda, County Louth, Republic of Ireland.
www.choicepublishing.ie

Paperback ISBN: 978-1-913275-93-8

A CIP catalogue record for this book is available from the National Library.

DEDICATION

This book is dedicated to Gerry Walsh K.S.G, former Director and *"Doc"* of the Belvedere Newsboys' Club, Dublin. He was one of the most influential leaders in this Club, leading and guiding young boys and men in a positive direction in their lives for over seventy years.

Contents

The Pigs Feet Murder

It was the little five-year-old girl, Eileen O'Flaherty, who saw it first. There it was, lying down at the bottom of the basement steps, inside an old empty tenement house that was in the early stages of collapsing in on itself. *"Oh, look at that"*, Eileen cried out as she pointed her little finger downwards. *"Look at what"?* asked her older impatient sister Kitty, who was holding her by the other hand. *"Down there"*, shouted Eileen. Their small gang of young friends were going out to the back yard of the old house to play games and they were all too intent on getting the game started to be bothered with looking down into a tenement basement. To keep Eileen quiet, Kitty looked down in the direction that she was pointing. Her eyes opened wide at what she saw down below. She then let out a roar to her pals who had gone ahead of her out into the backyard. *"Quick, come back, there's a great big doll down the stairs"*.

One by one, her friends came to have a look at what Eileen had seen. At first, they all agreed with Kitty that it was indeed a doll, after all it did look like one of those great big dolls they would often see posing in the window of Guiney's clothing shop and it still had all its clothes on as well.

As they slowly made their way down the steps to where it lay, the group of young children suddenly stopped in horrified silence, something just didn't seem right. From three steps away they realised that it might not be a doll. They all looked in terror at the outstretched corpse, with its head turned to one side and its eyes wide open, lying close to their feet in the semi darkness of the tenement basement. *"That's Mister Flynn who sells the Pig's Feet..."*. whispered Kathleen O'Shea *"...he must have fallen down here when he was drunk"*. *"Is he asleep or what"?* asked young Jimmy Bradley. Ten-year-old Kathleen bent down to get a closer look. *"I think he's dead"*, she answered. *"Oh, Holy God, we'd better tell someone quick"*, roared out Mary O'Sullivan, who took off back up the stairs screaming and crying with fright.

In next to no time at all, the stairway was filled with people from the neighbouring streets who had been alerted by the screams of Mary O'Sullivan, all pushing and shoving each other, all keen to get a look at what was going on. A woman at the top of the stairs called out, asking what had happened and a voice from down below suddenly shouted up, *"It's Pig's Feet Flynn, I think he's been shot in the head"*. When this news began to circulate amongst the mob that had gathered outside, all of the black shawled women knelt to the ground and taking out their Rosary Beads, began to pray.

Fifty-two-year-old Thomas *'Pigs Feet'* Flynn, was a short, slim build of a man from county Waterford who had a small shop near the corner of Purdon Street and Corporation Street, where he sold, amongst other things, Pigs Feet, hence the nick name "Pig's Feet" that he was given by the people in the area. At the outbreak of the First World War, Thomas Flynn had joined up with the Royal Dublin Fusiliers and had fought against the Germans in France. Thomas had been married once but his young wife died in childbirth along with their baby.

Most people in his neighbourhood were always a little wary of Thomas, because he always seemed to keep to himself whenever he was in Jack Meagher's pub, he'd sit on his own in a corner drinking from the one pint all night. From this vantage point Thomas could see all the comings and goings of the pub, some people were of the opinion that perhaps he suffered from some form of *'Shell Shock'*. Even in his little shop he would barely speak to anyone who went in to buy his hairy Pig's Feet.

The Dublin Metropolitan Police had been alerted to the find and soon arrived on the scene where *'Pig's Feet'* was lying dead. All of the neighbours who had gathered at the top of the basement stairs had quickly exited the building when they heard of the arrival of the police.

A lorry load of British Auxiliary soldiers drove at speed down the street and came to a screeching halt. Their Commanding Officer stood by the lorry waving his gun in the air and shouting out orders to his men in a grand English accent. The soldiers jumped down off the back of their lorry and stood in a semi-circle formation, with rifles at the ready, outside the doorway of the old and abandoned tenement house.

The Army Officer went inside and spoke to one of the policemen. The Officer explained that while they were passing through the area, they saw the crowd gathering and spotting a police uniform, thought they might be in need of some help. He then shouted out another order and two of his men headed inside and down the stairs to the basement. They soon came back out carrying poor *'Pig's Feet'* and placed him on the floor in the back of the lorry.

Soon enough, the soldiers and police were gone. A small group of curious neighbours went back in to the hallway to get a good look down at where the body had been found. The remains of *'Pig's Feet'* were brought to Jervis Street hospital for examination.

Sergeant Stone from Summerhill Police Station decided that he would make his way down to the scene of the crime and have a good look around for himself. He brought a young Constable with him to watch his back, just in case. He never did like the idea of carrying a firearm when he went out on foot patrol during the day but on this occasion, he thought, as an extra precaution, he would. He walked over to his desk and from a drawer he took out a fully loaded Webley and Scott .32 calibre pistol. He carefully fastened the gun belt around his waist and put the weapon into its holster. Dublin Castle had warned him to always wear his weapon when leaving the Station, no matter what the reason. Without his weapon he could become an easy target to a waiting gunman.

This was a very violent time in the history of Ireland. In the aftermath of the 1916 rising, Irishmen were more determined than ever to gain independence from British Rule. British Soldiers out on patrol and Policemen on the beat, became prime targets for ambush.

Although many of the members of the Police Force were Catholic, it never stopped them from being shot down in front of their families as they walked to Sunday Mass. Everywhere gunmen lurked in the shadows waiting for an opportunity to strike. Sergeant Stone was stationed in one of the most volatile areas of Dublin City.

The Sergeant and his companion took their time as they walked down Rutland Street and into Gloucester Street. They were in no hurry and he wanted to make their presence in these streets very noticeable. He wanted people to see and feel his presence, he was the law and the law had to be obeyed, whether people liked it or not.

They soon enough made their way to the scene of the

crime in the basement of the old tenement house. There were a few children nearby playing street games. While he noticed nobody standing around the street, he could certainly feel curious eyes staring out at him from every window of the tenement houses all along the street. The Sergeant knew that the people in this neighbourhood missed nothing of the goings on of the Police.

He told the Constable to stand guard at the doorway of the building and to make sure he wasn't disturbed. Sergeant Stone had a lot of experience of looking at dead bodies, he was no stranger to death. He had served in the police force in South Africa after the Boer Wars. He had indeed witnessed all types of crime and slaughter there. In his much younger years, he had spent time in London when Jack the Ripper was on the loose.

At the bottom of the stairs, he struck a match, the flame throwing up shadows along the wall and across the basement floor where the body of *"Pig's Feet"* was found by the young children. The Sergeant carefully examined the scene. He then walked slowly back up the stairs and examined the hand rail and steps. Pleased enough with what he saw, both he and his Constable headed back to their Station up on Summerhill.

The following morning Sergeant Stone and two young Constables made their way over to Jervis Street Hospital. The Sergeant wanted to talk to the Medical Examiner and hear his views on the cause of death of Thomas Flynn. It was of course, the responsibility of the detective unit in Dublin Castle to follow up on any suspicious deaths in the city but Sergeant Stone just wanted to make sure that everything was done by the book, after all, this murder happened on his patch.

On their arrival at the hospital the Sergeant made inquiries at the reception desk. The Medical Examiner, he was told, was expecting him. One of Constables was ordered to wait outside by the hospital door and the other was to follow the Sergeant. For that time of the morning the hospital seemed quite busy with nurses and doctors rushing to and fro. The young Constable was then told to stand guard outside of the Examiner's office.

The Sergeant knocked on the door and without waiting for a reply, walked straight in. The Medical Examiner, quite a rotund sort of man and much shorter in height than Sergeant Stone's six foot four inches, looked over his reading glasses and said *"Ah, Sergeant Stone, just the man. I have some results for you"*. The Sergeant was never sure what kind of reception to expect from the Medical Examiner, he always found him to be too moody for his liking. *"Very good, sir"*, the Sergeant replied. *"Now, first off..."* began the Examiner, *"...he wasn't shot through the head but he did however, die a violent death"*.

Sergeant Stone had already figured that out for himself the day before. In the light of the match, he noticed that there was no blood anywhere on the walls in the basement where the victim was found, nor were there any blood marks on the stair rail. If Flynn had been shot in the basement the noise from the gun would have echoed throughout the old building and most everyone in that street above would have heard it. It was too risky a place for a shooting. There was only a small amount of blood on the basement floor, nothing like what he would have expected to find if the murder had taken place there.

So why did *'Pig's Feet'* have to die? wondered the Sergeant as he waited for more details of the murder from the Medical Examiner. *"The back of his skull was crushed in. He was struck from behind, possibly with an iron bar or maybe a poker of some description and was probably dead before he even hit the ground,"* said the Examiner. *"I'll send my finished report into Dublin Castle as soon as it's ready and I'll make sure you get a copy also"*. The Sergeant thanked him and left.

In next to no time at all, word or rumour to be more precise, was soon out on the street that *'Pig's Feet'* was a paid informer, working in the shadows of Dublin Castle as a spy and that's why he was shot in the head by *'The Boys'*. That was how Sergeant Stone had heard it from one of his own informants and that's how he decided to leave it for the present.

A few days later however, he received notification that Dublin Castle *'have reached the conclusion that Thomas Flynn had died from falling down the steps of the tenement basement while he was drunk and had probably cracked open the back of his skull on one of the steps. This case is now considered closed'*. In his own mind, Sergeant Stone was of the opinion that Dublin Castle just couldn't be bothered investigating the death of Thomas Flynn, they probably considered him a nobody and not worth the effort. But he was of a different frame of mind and was determined to catch whoever was responsible for the murder, with or without the help of Dublin Castle.

On an unusually quiet day in the Station, Sergeant Stone was sitting at his desk, smoking his pipe, with a question on his mind. *"Who would want to kill Thomas Flynn?"* he thought, *"He was known in the neighbourhood as a quiet man who kept to himself, a harmless sort of a fella who had few if any friends at all"*. The Sergeant decided that the time had come for action.

So, with the assistance of his two Constables they headed down to Purdon Street and Flynn's shop. The Sergeant knew that Thomas Flynn lived in a couple of rooms up over the shop, he would check them out. The two Constables forced in the door of the shop with the help of an iron lever.

It was a very small shop with a large box of loose potatoes taking up all the space on the left-hand side and two sacks of onions and several heads of cabbage on the floor over on the other side.

Further in, there was a small plank of a counter sitting on top of two tall wooden crates. Up over this counter and hanging up on hooks reaching down from the low ceiling, were at least a dozen raw pig's feet and behind the shop door was a brown shop-coat belonging to Thomas Flynn, hanging from a nail.

To the Sergeant's trained eye, nothing seemed out of place. But he did notice that just in behind the counter was a narrow stairway leading up to the area above the shop. With one Constable on guard outside the door and the other Constable inside, Sergeant Stone made his way up the rickety stairs. He found one large room, divided in two by a curtain hanging over a long piece of rope reaching across from one side of the room to the other. On one side of the curtain, there was a single bed with a few coats and blankets thrown over it, a small dresser with a mirror on top and a pile of clothes thrown in a heap on the floor over by the one and only window in the room. He noticed too, a Crucifix on the wall up over the bed.

On the other side of the curtain was the makings of a small kitchen and eating area with one chair, a table and a small fireplace with a kettle next to it. On the table he saw a small piece of unlit candle sitting on a saucer, a teapot, a milk jug, a half bag of sugar and two tea cups. There were no other rooms or toilet upstairs.

The room showed no signs of a fight or a struggle, there was no blood to be seen anywhere and no weapon in sight. The Sergeant bent down slightly and looked out the one single window in the room. He had a clear view looking down into the narrow street below.

Across the road and over the boundary wall that ran the full length of Purdon Street, he found himself looking at the back of the Flats in Corporation Place. Feeling exasperated, Sergeant Stone felt he was no wiser now than when he first came into the shop but none the less, he did wonder why there were two tea cups on the table and who had been keeping Thomas Flynn company?

As he turned away from the window, the sunlight from outside, ever so slightly and gently, reflected back from underneath the bed and up into the Sergeants face. Kneeling down out of curiosity onto the dusty floor he put his head down and looked in under the bed. The first thing that he noticed was a large white piss-pot with the figure of a nude woman on the side, surrounded by blue and red flowers. His eyes then ever so slowly, moved across from the pot and there it was.

The Sergeant reached his hand in under the bed and gently lifted out the little object that had caught the sunlight from the window. It was a woman's earring. The Sergeant put it in his tunic pocket and smiled. He then headed back down the small stairway and out onto the street. Having then secured the door of the premises, the three policemen returned to their Station up on Summerhill.

Lily Holohan and Biddy Lane were two well-seasoned prostitutes. At 43 years old, Lily was the eldest of the two,

13

Biddy was a much younger woman at 29 years of age. Both women looked at least ten years older than they actually were. Lily originally came from the Curragh in County Kildare. Her father was a soldier but she never knew which of all the soldiers in the Curragh was her father. As a child, whenever she asked her mother which one was her father, she was told, *"Take your pick"*. At fourteen years of age, Lily had made her own way to Dublin and sold herself on its streets in order to survive.

From the time Biddy Lane was a new born baby, she was being brought up by the Nun's. They had her baptised as Bridget Lane because she was found abandoned in a lane off Beaver Street on Saint Bridget's Day. She too, ended up, at thirteen years of age, selling herself on the streets.

These two women sat huddled close together in the snug of O'Reilly's pub on the corner of Corporation Street and Railway Street, sipping a glass of whiskey each, the air between them was tense. Lily glared across at Biddy and warned her,

"You had better keep your trap shut or you'll end up the same way he did, I'm tellin' yeah that now". Keeping her head down low and crying into her drink, Biddy was unable to contain herself any longer and burst out *"But I can't stop*

thinkin' about it, I'm tellin' yeah, I can't even sleep". Lily hit her a swift and stinging clatter on the side of her face. Biddy almost choked from trying to stifle the scream that wanted to come out of her mouth.

"Now..." scowled Lily, *"...you had better listen to me and listen very carefully because I have no intention of swinging from a rope in Mountjoy Jail because of your mouth".* Poor Biddy found it hard to concentrate on anything other than the stinging sensation that she felt coming from the side of her face. After taking a sip of whiskey out of her glass, Lily whispered across the table, *"We'll have to go up to Polly Foster's Shebeen in Killarney Street and talk to Jack O'Donnell and his pal, Charlie McLoughlin, maybe they'll know what to say in case the Rozzers come snooping around. Now, stop your sniffling and get another drink in".*

Sergeant Stone lived up over the Police Station on Summerhill, he had the use of two rooms and a toilet. There was a third room next to the toilet that was used by any new Constables sent up to him from the countryside, somewhere for them to stay until they got settled in. At the moment it was empty.

There were times when the Sergeant would often feel a little bit lonely living on his own. He remembered there was a young woman one time who took his fancy alright, Annie Joyce was her name. She was originally from County Sligo and worked for a doctor over on the South Circular Road. In the early days the Sergeant knew that his working hours would never suit their courtship.

He remembered being told, when he first joined the Police Force, that he must never consider himself as being off duty. Whenever Annie wanted to go out dancing, he was always going on duty or because of the violent political situation throughout the country, he was always looking over his shoulder in case someone decided to take a pot shot at him. Annie didn't like that idea at all, she wanted a quiet life and they soon parted company. She later married the doctor she had been working for.

Sergeant Stone sat up late into the night, studying and turning the earring around in his fingers. *"How in the Devil's name did a woman's earring find its way underneath the bed of Thomas Flynn"?* That was the question going round and round inside his head. It was a white coloured, pearl-drop earring with a silver back to it and it had a hook coming out at the top. *"Whatever woman owns this piece of jewellery has to have a hole in her ear to hang tat hook through"* he said out loudly to himself.

The Sergeant had worked in this area of Dublin for the past five years and had made a point from day one, of getting to know the whole patch of it inch by inch, He knew every hook and crook that walked its streets by sight and smell. But the Sergeant had no memory, in all those five years, of ever seeing Thomas Flynn with a woman on his arm, let alone a woman in his bedroom. And this was no ordinary cheap earring that he'd found, a pair of earrings like this, he reckoned, cost quite a bit of money.

Lily Holohan and Biddy Lane held on to each other as they walked along Killarney Street, there was a light drizzle of rain coming down and a cold breeze blowing at their back. When they came to Polly Foster's Shebeen, Lily reached out and gave a hard rapping knock on the window. The side of a curtain was pulled back ever so slightly and a pair of eyes looked out into the darkness of the night. When the door was opened, they were greeted by the smell of stale drink and cigarette smoke.

The place was quiet because it was mid-week and a bit early in the night for customers. The room that they were shown into at the back of the house had a table standing in the middle of the room surrounded by several chair, on one side of the room was a well-worn and well used sofa with a torn blanket thrown over the back of it. In one corner and at an angle, was a counter with drinking glasses on it, the room was similar in looks to a small pub. The Shebeen was downstairs and the Brothel was upstairs.

The owner of the premises was Polly Foster. She was in her early sixties, she was rough, tough and hard as nails. Polly was born in Ash Street over on the southside of the city and like her mother before her, she too spent most of her life involved in Prostitution. Polly was a peroxide blonde who wore ruby red lipstick across her mouth. She was a little under five feet in height and weighed no less than ten stone. Polly always carried a cut-throat razor on her person which was concealed beneath her skirt and held in place by one of her garters.

Throughout her many years of running Brothels and Shebeens, Polly Foster had many an occasion where she had to produce the razor in order to stress a point or two with a disgruntled sailor or to keep a young prostitute in line. Jack O'Donnell and Charlie McLoughlin worked for Polly, they were her two *"Heavies",* who knew how to handle themselves in any given situation. They were always there to carry out Polly's orders.

Jack O'Donnell, at forty-two years of age, was tall and

lean with a long skinny face and dark vicious eyes. He always wore a cap on his head and a scarf wrapped tightly around his neck and stuffed inside his waistcoat. Jack had a great big heavy moustache that hung down over his top lip and almost covered his entire mouth. He was certainly no stranger to violence, having spent most of his younger life in and out of Mountjoy Jail for beating up prostitutes and handling stolen goods. He lived by his wits, he was born on the streets and reared on the streets, never knowing any father or mother.

His sidekick, thirty-five-year-old, Charlie McLoughlin, was slightly shorter than Jack. Charlie had a nasty looking scar running across his chin, just beneath his bottom lip, the result of a barroom brawl with two cattlemen. He had spent five years of his younger life locked up in Kilmainham Jail for setting fire to a warehouse full of cattle hides. As a result of this fire one man lost his life.

Jack and Charlie sat themselves over at one side of the table, while Lily and Biddy sat opposite. They all sat in silence while waiting for Polly Foster to come into the room and seat herself down at the head of the table. Suddenly and without warning, Polly's voice roared out all over the house *"Carrie, where's the tea"?* Then she appeared standing in the doorway of the room with her hands on her hips. She scowled across at Jack O'Donnell and said *"You'd need to knock some manners into that Young One Jack, she's getting worse ever since you-know-what"*. Jack sat back in his chair and while stretching his legs out and scratching his head, answered Polly. *"As long as she keeps her mouth shut and says nothing to the Police, she's grand, otherwise she'll go the same way, no matter what age she is"*.

Carrie Thompson was sixteen years old and since leaving school at fourteen was working as a prostitute under the guidance of Polly Foster. She lived in fear of Polly and Jack O'Donnell, they would often beat her for no good reason. One time Polly threw her down the stairs of the brothel because Carrie dared to answer her back, she didn't like back-chat from any of her girls. Carrie had natural blonde hair and blue eyes.

Carrying a tray of five cups of tea into the room, Carrie put the tray down on the table and then sat on a low stool over in the corner of the room by the back window. She had been warned that she was there to listen and not to talk. Polly had told her that she was to give everyone tea and not to give out any alcohol unless it was paid for in advance.

Lily Holohan was the first to break the silence in the room.

"So, what's the plan now..."? she asked as she looked at Polly. *"...they have the body"* she said. Charlie McLoughlin laughed out loud at her question. *"Yes, they have the body alright..."* he repeated after her *"... but it was 'The Boys' who shot him for informing on them. Well, that's what I made sure to tell everyone and that's what they all believe happened. 'Pig's Feet' was an informer, end of story.*

Sitting up straight in his chair and having taken a dagger out of a case strapped to his leg, Jack O'Donnell gave out a stern warning in a slow and chilling voice, *"That's the plan and if anyone in this room says any different, they too will end up in a tenement basement, just like Pig's Feet did. Do I make myself clear?"*. He slowly turned his head and looked across the room at Carrie Thompson. Ever since the night of the murder, Polly Foster had warned Carrie that she was not to go outdoors without her say so. Jack then looked across the table and staring into the face of Biddy Lane and raising his voice, screamed out, *"Do I make myself Clear"?* He then stabbed his knife with great force into the table, causing everyone to jump with fright.

The following Saturday night, two of Sergeant Stone's Constables herded a very noisy group of seven drunken women into the Police Station. One of the Constables was barking out orders to the group of women. *"Now ladies, straight ahead and into the empty cell on the left"* he shouted. *"You can't arrest me…"* one of the women shouted at him *"…my husband died fighting for the King"*. Another woman looked at her and said *"Who was that man you were reefing the hair out of down in the pub, was he not your husband"*? The first woman answered in a subdued tone *"Well, he was supposed to die for the King but he turned around and ran away instead"*. The whole Station erupted into roars of laughter.

Sergeant Stone stood up from his desk and towering over the group of women said in a gentle voice. *"Now, ladies, please do as you're told by my Constable"*. The group of women shuffled past the Sergeant towards the open cell door. As the last woman passed by Sergeant Stone, she gave a slight tug on his sleeve. He looked down at her, puzzled as to why she was doing this, she then sat down on a chair by the desk pretending to fix her shoe.

Curiosity got the better of the Sergeant, and so he knelt down on the floor pretending to help with her shoe and as he did so, she whispered ever so quietly into his ear, *"I know who killed Pig's Feet"*. He quickly lifted his head up in surprise and looked at her. The woman stood up from the

22

chair and making sure that all her friends could hear, she said *"Thank you Sergeant, it's fixed now"* and following the rest of her pals, she walked into the open cell.

The Sergeant had a restless sleep that night. He spent most of the time staring up at the bedroom ceiling, asking himself over and over again, *"Did that woman really say that, does she really know who killed Thomas Flynn and if so, how does she know"?* Because of his restless night, the Sergeant overslept the following morning. One of his Constables came knocking on his bedroom door and woke him up. After a wash and a shave and a cup of tea, he eventually came down into the Station area.

A young Constable, looking up from his desk and pointing towards the cell full of hung-over women, asked the Sergeant, *"What will I do with this lot"*. The Sergeant answered, *"Take down their details and send them all home"*. As the women filed out of the cell past the Sergeant, the woman that had whispered into his ear the night before was sitting in the cell, fiddling with her shoe. *"This bloody shoe is a nuisance and I can't fix it right"* she shouted after her friends. *"Don't worry Annie..."*, one of her friends shouted back at her, *"...we'll see you later"*.

When her friends were gone out onto the street, Annie put

her shoe on and as she was passing by the Sergeant's desk something caught her eye and she looked down. She then looked up at the Sergeant and said in a low voice, *"That's her and you'll know where to find me"*. The woman walked out of the Police Station. The Sergeant reached out his hand and picking up the Pearl-Drop earring from off his desk, slipped it back into his pocket for safe keeping.

Carrie Thompson was still very upset over the death of Thomas Flynn. She hated Polly Foster and her two thugs, Jack O'Donnell and Charlie McLoughlin, for killing Thomas. She remembered one day in particular, just before the previous Christmas, when she walked into his shop. She had been ordered by Polly that morning to go to Thomas's shop and to bring home half a dozen Pig's Feet. She remembered standing in the little shop and Thomas speaking to her, she was surprised because he had never spoken to her before.

At first, she thought that he was just muttering to himself but then he repeated himself and said *"I can help you, if you'll let me"*. She didn't understand, what did he mean by that, he could help her, help her how? As he handed her twelve Pig's Feet wrapped up in newspaper, he told her to make sure to come back in to his shop the following day. For some time now Thomas Flynn had noticed the pretty young blonde girl who came into his shop almost daily and how she was being used and abused by the Brothel Madam, Polly Foster.

Thomas thought back to all those years ago when he had fallen in love with a sweet sixteen-year-old girl from Dungarvan in County Waterford and she too had pretty blonde hair. They walked up the aisle together on the day of her eighteenth birthday, he was the luckiest man in the world. Twelve months later she died from complications giving birth and their new born baby girl died as well.

It was after their funeral that Thomas decided to leave the place of his birth and join the war. He never went back to Dungarvan, even now, after all these years, he could still feel the heartache and the heartbreak of losing the love of his life. He settled in Dublin instead, hoping to lose himself in amongst the crowded streets.

He did however, keep in touch with his younger sister, Eileen who still lived in the home place just outside Dungarvan town, they would often send each other Christmas cards and that. In more recent times however, he had written her a letter telling her about Carrie Thompson and how he would like to help her escape from the clutches of the Madam. His plan was to help Carrie escape to Dungarvan and to stay with Eileen until something could be worked out for her.

Carrie never mentioned a word of this to anyone. Some nights she would manage to slip out of the Brothel on some pretence or other and under cover of darkness, she would visit Thomas. They would sit upstairs over his shop, drinking tea and talking by the fireside about his plans. One night he handed Carrie a small fancy coloured box and told her he would like her to have it for her birthday. When she opened it up, she gasped in surprise, her two blue eyes brightened up more than ever before as she looked down at a beautiful pair of pure white Pearl-Drop earrings. Thomas explained that they were all that he had left of his wife's jewellery and that he wished for Carrie to have them.

Some days later, while Sergeant Stone was lost in thought gazing out of the Station window, one of his Constables stepped up beside him and said, *"Here you are Sergeant, here's that list of names and information that you asked me to type up for you"*. The Sergeant took the list and sat down at his desk to check it out. As he read down the page, he stopped at one name in particular and then called his Constable over.

"What's this name here"? he asked. *"Oh..."* answered the Constable, *"...that's Annie Rogers, the woman who had the broken shoe, you remember that woman you helped? Well, she told me her name is Annie Rogers and said that she worked in the Stew House at the top of Buckingham Street, she insisted that I put the word 'Earring' after her name for some strange reason and so I did".* The Sergeant looked at the name and knew that he would have to talk to this woman, Annie Rogers and find out what she knew about the murder of Thomas Flynn.

Later that same day two detectives arrived at the Station asking to see Sergeant Stone. When he heard his name being mentioned he looked out through the open door of his office and knew straightaway that they were from Dublin Castle. With the office door eventually closed behind them the taller of the two detectives spoke out. *"We believe Sergeant, that you are still looking into a supposed murder case that we have already shut down..."* he said, *"...that of Thomas Flynn. Is that correct"?* The Sergeant sat upright in his seat with a determined look on his face, *"That is certainly correct..."* he answered, *"Flynn was murdered on my patch and I'm within a hairs breath of catching his killer or killers, as the case may be".*

The second detective, while removing his hat and placing it down on the Sergeant's desk said *"That's great news Sergeant and we're glad to hear that. Well done, however..."* he said with a hesitation in his voice, *"...all murder cases come under the jurisdiction of Dublin Castle, so therefore..."* it was at this point that his companion cut across him. *"What my friend here is trying to say Sergeant is that, given the circumstances, we'd very much like to be involved in this case and so, we would appreciate it if you would send us over a written update on what you've uncovered and I'm sure we can help each other out"*. As the two detectives left the Station the Sergeant knew that he had little or no choice in the matter.

The Sergeant knew that he had to talk to Annie Rogers and the sooner the better but how was he going to achieve this? It would have to be done in private and very quietly too because if she was found out her life would be in danger and she too could end up like *'Pig's Feet'*. After giving some thought to the situation, he came up with an idea, he would seek the help of one of the Nuns who ran the Soup Kitchen where Annie worked. He had recently met the Mother Superior during some court case or other where a couple of young girls were up on a charge of stealing money out of a collection box in the nearby church. He felt sure that he could trust the Mother Superior to keep things under wrap.

Annie Rogers was originally from City Quay and was married to Jimmy. They had two sons who had both emigrated to Australia. Jimmy worked as a foreman in one of the big coal yards on Sir John Rogerson's Quay, over on the southside of the River Liffey. One Friday, Jimmy had spotted two temporary coalmen stealing the wages money out of the company's office in the yard where he worked. He reported them straightaway and they were later arrested but the stolen money was never recovered and so they were released.

Some weeks later Jimmy was making his way home from his local pub after having a few pints after work. As he passed by a laneway a hand reached out and dragged him down into the lane where two men beat him up. Three days later Jimmy Rogers died as a result of the beating. His wife Annie was convinced that they were the same two men that had committed the robbery in the coal yard, Jimmy had told her their names, Jack O'Donnell and Charlie McLoughlin.

In her capacity as Cook in the Stew House, each day Annie Rogers would go out and arrange the purchase of whatever was needed for that day's dinner. On one particular day

Annie walked into Purdon Street from Corporation Street on her way to work. As she passed by the doorway of Thomas Flynn's shop, she could hear him coughing and gasping for breath. Thinking he was in serious trouble Annie went inside to see what assistance she could offer the poor man.

She saw Thomas sitting on the floor behind the counter. *"Are you alright there, Mister Flynn"?* she called out to him. He couldn't get enough breath out of his lungs to answer. She made her way in behind the counter and helped him up the stairway to his room. She told him to get into his bed while she made him a cup of tea. He told her that he hadn't eaten in a week because he was never well enough to cook something for himself.

Annie Rogers left Mister Flynn in his bed and walking out onto Purdon Street, closed the shop door behind her. A half hour later she was back with a Billy Can filled with hot stew for him. She let herself into the shop and brought the stew up the stairs to him.

The two of them later came to an arrangement that Annie would bring him his dinner each day and he would pay her for doing so. One day, in confidence, he told Annie of his plan to rescue Carrie Thompson and he showed her the Pearl-Drop earrings that he planned on giving to Carrie for her birthday.

Sergeant Stone met up with the Mother Superior and explained his situation to her. She said that she would make arrangements for him to speak in private to Annie Rogers the following day. When they finally met up Annie made sure to let the Sergeant know how she felt let down by the Police in relation to the death of her husband. She told him that she had deliberately brought her drunken women friends out onto the street to cause a scene, knowing that they'd be arrested and brought to his Station and by doing that she was able to make contact with the Sergeant without anyone being suspicious.

She then told him all that she knew about Thomas Flynn, how she became friends with him and of his plan to rescue Carrie Thompson. Annie also made sure to mention the Pearl-Drop earrings. Sergeant Stone asked Annie if she knew where Carrie was hiding out. She then gave him the name and address of Polly Foster who lived in Killarney Street.

She told him that Polly and her gang are always at that address on Friday nights. Before they parted company Annie stood up before the big tall Policeman and said *"Nobody is to know of my involvement in this, nobody"*. The Sergeant looked down at Annie and told her *"Don't worry, you have my word on that Misses Rogers"*.

After his updated report on the inquiries into the death of Thomas Flynn were sent over to Dublin Castle, Sergeant Stone just had to sit tight and wait for further instructions. In the meantime, he decided to check out where the premises of Polly Foster and her gang were located. He wanted to familiarise himself with the area around where the house was and to check out any possible escape routes that could be taken in the event of a raid by Dublin Castle.

He brought one of his young Constables out with him and made it look like it was a regular patrol of the streets, which he often did two or three times a week. They walked up Summerhill and turning right into Portland Row, they headed downhill in the direction of the Five Lamps. At the bottom of this street, they turned right into Killarney Street.

The Sergeant had instructed his Constable to keep a sharp eye out for anything unusual and to make a mental note of it. The street seemed quiet with several people passing up and down but nothing out of the ordinary. A little further on down the street the Sergeant noticed a young blonde headed girl standing on a chair and reaching up as she cleaned one of the windows on the outside of the house they were passing by. Nothing unusual about that he thought to himself.

As the young girl was attempting to get down off the chair however, something caught the Sergeants eye, she was wearing a Pearl-Drop earring in her right ear, the match of the one he had safely put away in his pocket. He took a second quick glance at the girl, that's her, he said to himself. It was then that a small plump, blonde headed older woman appeared from inside the house. She was accompanied by two men that Sergeant Stone recognised immediately from the description that Annie Rogers had earlier given him of Jack O'Donnell and Charlie McLoughlin. The woman shouted at the young girl, *"Carrie, get inside, you can finish that later"*. She gave the two police officers a cutting look and walked back into the house.

The Sergeant now had a good clear mental picture of what Carrie Thompson looked like as well as the three others who ran the Brothel. He also now knew the exact location of the Brothel that Annie Rogers had spoken to him about. And he was sure that the older woman with the peroxide blonde hair was most likely the Madam, Polly Foster.

As they walked back towards the Station, the Sergeant updated the young Constable on what was happening in relation to the Thomas Flynn murder investigation. When the two policemen eventually arrived back at Summerhill the Constable pulled out a street map of the area. *"Sergeant..."* he called out, *"...you might want to look at this"*.

Sergeant Stone walked over and standing next to the Constable, the two of them looked down at the map. The Constable pointed at the map and said *"This is where that house is located where we saw the young girl standing on the chair and there is a laneway running along at the back of that entire block of houses, a possible backdoor escape route for anyone wishing to avoid arrest",* he explained. *"Well done, Constable, we'd best keep that in mind. I'll make a proper Policeman out of you yet"* he joked, they both laughed.

Sergeant Stone met in secret on a few more occasions with Annie Rogers, giving her an update on his progress and strangely enjoying her company. She seemed very relaxed with him and spoke openly of perhaps someday joining her two sons in Australia. He told her that his family had originally come to Ireland during the Ulster Plantation of the 1600's. They were Lowland Scottish Presbyterian people, he explained. He told her that he had only one sister, Lily, who lived in Liverpool and was married to a Policeman, he said that Lily ran a large Boarding House over there. As they were saying their goodbyes, Annie reached out her hand and placing it ever so gently on the Sergeant's arm, looked up into his face and said, *"You mind yourself and take care"*.

A few days later word had come through to the Station on Summerhill, a directive from Dublin Castle. A raid on the Brothel in Killarney Street was planned for midnight on the following Friday night and all officers were to be fully armed. Uniformed personnel from both Summerhill Station and Store Street Station were to be involved as well as a unit of armed detectives from Dublin Castle.

Sergeant Stone gathered all of his staff around him and explained the situation. *"I don't want any heroics from any of you lads..."* he warned them. *"...leave that up to those detectives from the Castle, that's what they're paid for. Now, do I make myself clear"?* Sergeant Stone wanted to find Annie Rogers and tell her what was about to take place but he knew that he couldn't take the risk of making contact with her outside of their agreed schedule.

On Friday night Polly Foster stood in the corner of the room with a great big grin on her lipstick painted face. She knew from experience that drunken men and their money were easily parted when a young woman was thrown into the mix. Across the room Carrie Thompson sat on the lap of a well-known local politician who was well and truly drunk and singing out at the top of his voice. Two older women, Lily Holohan and Biddy Lane were busy entertaining two country gentlemen they had picked up in a pub on Amiens Street.

The bedrooms upstairs were fully occupied with more girls and their clients. Polly laughed out loud at the noise coming down through the ceiling, *'The more noise, the more money'* she thought to herself. On either side of Polly stood Jack O'Donnell and Charlie McLoughlin.

Approaching midnight, the entire block of houses was quietly surrounded by armed police. The detective unit would make an entry into the house from the front and back doors simultaneously. Anyone who escaped from the house would be apprehended by those police officers waiting outside.

They were all under orders and told that if anyone came out shooting, they were to be killed on-sight. Sergeant Stone was to assist the detective unit because he could identify the two men the detectives were most interested in arresting, they wanted to take them alive if at all possible. The Sergeant was ordered to enter the house with his weapon drawn and at the ready.

Polly Foster wasn't sure what the noise was she had just heard or where it was coming from. She told Charlie McLoughlin to throw a check on the front door. As he was halfway down the hall the door came crashing in on top of him and knocked him to the floor. Immediately, Polly looked out into the hallway and without any hesitation let out a roar, *"It's a raid, it's the Rozzers"*.

Panic swept through the entire downstairs part of the house as the back door too came crashing in. Two detectives handcuffed McLoughlin and led him out to the front of the house. Polly tried to make a run for it but was soon lifted up off her feet by two big burley Policemen.

Sergeant Stone and his two detective friends stood at the entrance into the room where the drinking had been taking place, with their guns at the ready. They soon stopped dead in their tracks as they looked across the room at the face of a very frightened Carrie Thompson. Standing with his back against the wall of the room was Jack O'Donnell with Carrie Thompson standing in front of him. He had one hand placed on her forehead, forcing her head back and exposing her throat. With his other hand he held a long sharp knife across her neck. *"Come any closer and I'll kill her..."* he warned

37

the three lawmen. *"...I'll slit her throat right open if any of you make a wrong move. Now lay down your weapons on the floor"*, he ordered. The two detectives did as they were told.

However, Sergeant Stone hesitated in doing so. Looking O'Donnell in the eye he slowly raised his loaded weapon to a firing position. Everyone in the room froze, nobody moved or uttered a sound, Sergeant Stone held his nerve. The silence was shattered by a roaring laugh from Jack O'Donnell. *"Go on Copper..."* he jeered, *"...you haven't got the guts"*. The Sergeant's trigger finger pulled backwards ever so slowly; the gun exploded. Carrie Thompson screamed out and fainted to the floor. The bullet ripped into O'Donnell's right shoulder, shattering bone and tearing muscle apart. The force of the shot pinning him even further in against the wall and his now lifeless arm dropped his knife to the floor. He stood there in agonising pain, a shocked look on his face.

Without taking his eyes of O'Donnell, the Sergeant gave an order to the two detectives, *"Get him outta here"*. He then walked over and carefully picked Carrie Thompson up off the floor. The uniform Constabulary began rounding up all of the other occupants of the house. The local politician was protesting his innocence, telling one of the young Constables that he was hoodwinked into going to the Brothel.

The Green Street courthouse trial received tremendous publicity in all of the newspapers in Ireland, England and was even mentioned in some American Newspapers. In order to save their own necks, Polly Foster and Charlie McLoughlin had both turned King's Evidence against Jack O'Donnell, this meant that they would get a reduced sentence each. Lily Holohan and Biddy Lane were offered a reduced prison sentence also if they too informed on O'Donnell.

Sergeant Stone was first to be called to give his account of events. He told the packed courtroom that Thomas Flynn's plan to help get Carrie Thompson escape out of Dublin was discovered by Polly Foster and Jack O'Donnell when they saw Thompson wearing a pair of expensive Pearl-Drop earrings. They forced Carrie to tell them where she got them from. The three of them, along with Charlie McLoughlin, Lily Houlihan and Biddy Lane made their way to Flynn's shop late one night. When Thomas Flynn heard Carrie Thompson's voice from outside, he opened the door.

The gang forced Thomas Flynn up the stairs to his room

where the two men threw him onto the bed and began to beat him up. As Carrie Thompson attempted to pull the two thugs up off Thomas Flynn, one of them threw a punch at her and knocked her to the floor, one of her Pearl-Drop earrings fell from her ear and rolled in under the bed.

Polly Foster and her two female companions searched around the room for money, they found a small amount of cash under a clock on the Mantel Piece up over the fireplace. Polly Foster emptied the money into her pocket.

Jack O'Donnell then dragged Thomas Flynn up off the bed and pulled him in behind the curtain that divided the room in two. He pushed Thomas onto a chair next to the table. He told Charlie McLoughlin to give Thomas a few more punches until he told them where he kept the rest of his money. Thomas refused to speak or to say where his money was kept. Jack O'Donnell was standing by the fireplace behind the chair where Thomas Flynn was seated.

In a fit of rage, O'Donnell picked up a metal poker from beside the fireplace and turning around, struck several blows to the back of Thomas Flynn's head. Thomas let out a grunt and slumping forward fell dead to the floor. Carrie Thompson and the three older women stood looking in shocked silence. On the word of O'Donnell, the women cleaned up the blood on the floor. They all left the shop and headed back to the Brothel.

The Sergeant said that according to a statement made by Charlie McLoughlin, the next day it was decided that they would all return to the shop later that night and that both he and Jack O'Donnell would get rid of the body. The women would all help to fix the room up so that there were no signs of a fight or anything else. On their way back to the Brothel the two men threw the body of Thomas Flynn down into the basement of the old tenement house where the young children found it the next day.

In his statement McLoughlin said that he was the one who had started off the rumour about Flynn being an informer so as to throw people off the scent. The Sergeant then went on to tell McLoughlin's version of the cash robbery that had taken place in the Coal Yard and how he witnessed Jack McDonnell beat up Jimmy Rogers in the laneway and how they had left him for dead. The Sergeant knew that McLoughlin had failed to mention his own part in the beating.

The Sergeant, quoting from McLoughlin's statement, told the Judge that the two men made off with the stolen money. Later that night they both sat in a pub down by the Docks and had several large glasses of whiskey, paid for by the stolen money. When they woke up in the doorway of the pub the next morning the remainder of the stolen money was gone, the robbers had been robbed.

The next person to testify to the Court was Carrie Thompson. In Green Street Courthouse there is a long table situated down on the floor facing the Judge. On top of this table is placed a chair and it is on this chair that each witness must sit when addressing the Judge. Because Carrie Thompson was small in height the Court Clerk had to help her up onto the table. The Judge asked Carrie to please speak up so that he could hear her clearly and to start at the beginning. He cautioned all of those present in the courtroom to remain absolutely silent.

Carrie began by telling the Judge that she was an only child and that when she was ten years old her poor mother had died from Consumption. She spoke out and told the Judge of how her father struggled at the loss of his wife. He had worked in a Flour Mill for most of his life and because the dust from the Flour affected his lungs, he eventually had to give up his job. Finding it hard to make ends meet financially her father had turned to a Money Lender for help. That Money Lender was Polly Foster.

A few days after burying her father Carrie received a visit from Polly Foster and Jack O'Donnell. Polly told Carrie that she would have to come and work for her because her father still owed money on what he had borrowed. Carrie told the Judge that she was then only fourteen years of age.

Carrie said that she refused to work in a Brothel and it was then that Jack O'Donnell beat her to within an inch of her life. He then dragged her through the streets to the Brothel and gave her another beating. The Court Clerk stood up and apologising to the Judge, handed Carrie a handkerchief to wipe away her tears. At this stage most of the people in the courtroom were also in tears as, Carrie then finished her testimony by telling the Judge of the first day that Thomas Flynn approached her about running away and escaping from the Brothel and of the beautiful Pearl-Drop earrings that he had given her. The Judge thanked Carrie and allowed her to return to her seat.

Annie Rogers was next called to the witness chair. Sergeant Stone accompanied Annie up to the long table and helped her up onto the chair, he then returned to his seat next to Carrie Thompson. Annie sat in the chair holding a large money box on her lap.

She told the Judge of the terrible beating that was inflicted on her poor defenceless husband some days after the robbery of the money from the Coal Yard. Her husband had told Annie the name of the two men involved, Jack O'Donnell and Charlie McLoughlin. She then told the Judge of how she helped Thomas Flynn when she found him lying sick on the floor of his shop and of how he eventually confided in her about his plan to rescue Carrie Thompson.

Annie told the packed courtroom of the reason why Polly Foster and her gang failed to find any money belonging to Thomas Flynn. It was because he had entrusted his money to Annie and asked her to keep it safe and if things should go wrong to make sure to give it to Carrie Thompson, in the hope that she would use it to begin a new life for herself. Annie then held the Cash Box that was sitting on her lap, high above her head and told the Judge it once belonged to Thomas Flynn.

A great big cry shattered the silence of the courtroom as Carrie Thompson stood up and screamed out in pain. This seemed to give licence to everyone elsc in the room to do the same. Sergeant Stone stood up and lifting Carrie Thompson up in his arms and with the permission of the Judge, led her out into the hallway of the courthouse. He nodded to a group of Constables to make a passageway clear for them. As they both sat together, surrounded by several Constables, a woman approached and standing before them, introduced herself as Eileen, the younger sister of Thomas Flynn.

On the day of sentencing, the judge placed a black cloth on his head and looking over his glasses at Jack O'Donnell pronounced the sentence of *'Death by Hanging'*. Sergeant Stone, looked up at O'Donnell, who was visibly shaken at the thought of facing the *'Hangman's Rope'* and nodded in approval at the final outcome of this horrendous case. Charlie McLoughlin was sentenced to eight years with Hard Labour, Polly Foster was given six years, Lily Houlihan and Biddy Lane were each sentenced to four years, all with Hard Labour. *"Take them down"* ordered the judge.

The following day Sergeant Stone invited Annie Rogers, Eileen Flynn and Carrie Thompson to join him for lunch in the Metropole Hotel. As they sat around the table, the Sergeant told them that he was worried about the safety of Carrie if she were to remain in Dublin.

He said that he had been in touch with his sister in Liverpool and that she suggested that Carrie could go and work for her. She would have a safe place to live and a job as well. Eileen reached across the table and placing her hand on Carrie's arm said, *"Now Carrie, here's a chance for you to make a great future for yourself. It's what my brother Tom would have wanted for you but it's up to you to decide"*. Carrie looked up at Annie Rogers and asked her *"Should I go Annie"?*

Annie told her that there was no safe future for her here in Dublin and that Liverpool sounded like a good option. It was then that Sergeant Stone surprised them all when he suggested *"Annie, why don't you go with her? There's nothing to hold you here and I mentioned you to my sister as well and sure she said you'd be more than welcome, and sure can't you both stay in the spare room up over the Station until you're ready to go"*. The three women sat with their mouths open, they couldn't believe what they had just heard and what was to be decided on. Reaching out, Annie joined hands with Eileen and Carrie and looking across the table at the Sergeant answered, *"Sure why not"*?

And so, the Sergeant's plan was put into operation. Eileen had headed back home to Dungarven with a promise from Carrie that she would write to her from Liverpool. One week later a Cab and Driver waited in Summerhill Place, a narrow lane behind the Police Station, to secretly whisk away to the boat, Sergeant Stone and the two women. The Sergeant had two of his Constables manage the luggage onto the carriage.

The Sergeant glanced up at the Driver of the carriage and was sure that he recognised him from somewhere but being too preoccupied with the task in hand of getting the two women off safely, dismissed the thought. The Driver however, recognised the Sergeant, even though he was out of uniform.

When they arrived at Amiens Street train station the trio quickly made their way onto the platform. But just before boarding the train however, the Sergeant took one more glance back over his shoulder at the Cab Driver and suddenly recognised him as Whiskers O'Toole, a known active member of the Fenian Movement. It was then that the Sergeant remembered that he was unarmed, despite the warning from Dublin Castle.

As the train pulled out of the station the excitement of the day was almost too much. The Sergeant could hardly believe he was seated in a railway carriage with Annie and Carrie, heading out along the coast to Dunlaoghaire and the boat, waiting to take the two women to England. With a smile on his face, the Sergeant took out an envelope from his inside breast pocket. *"Now..."* he announced, *"...I have some good news to share with you both..."*.

When he felt he had their total and undivided attention he held up a letter which he had received that very morning from Dublin Castle. *"...I have here a letter from the Castle. I am being promoted to the position of Police Inspector and transferred to a nice little Station out in the seaside town of Bray in County Wicklow. And it's from there, in two years' time, that I will retire from the Force on full pension. Now is that good news or what"* The two women cheered and danced around the carriage with delight.

Arriving in Dunlaoghaire the three of them stood waiting for the signal for Carrie and Annie to board the boat. They were all feeling a sense of excitement and sadness. The Sergeant stood there not too sure what to say or do. Then suddenly out of nowhere the boat's whistle let out a shrill cry. A voice then shouted out, *"All aboard that's going aboard"*.

Carrie told the Sergeant to bend down so that she could give him a farewell kiss on his cheek. Annie reached out her hand to shake goodbye and say thank you to the Sergeant. Their eyes locked and almost hesitating, the Sergeant held on to Annie's hand and asked *"Annie, will you marry me"*? He couldn't believe he had just said that. Annie looked at him and with a great big smile on her face said, *"I thought you'd never ask, but when"*? He began to stutter in his reply, *"In two years' time when I retire. I'll travel over to Liverpool and we can get married and buy a place of our own over there"*. And so, the boat pulled away from the pier and headed out over the Irish Sea.

Sergeant Stone had never felt quite like this before. He was all excited at the prospect of a future with Annie, his upcoming promotion to Inspector and his move to Bray. He reckoned he was the happiest man in the world. And so, with all of that excitement going around in his head he soon fell asleep as the train rolled along its tracks and back to Dublin.

Sergeant Stone woke with a jolt as the train eventually came to a halt in Amiens Street train station. He got to his feet and put on his hat and overcoat before stepping down out of the carriage. His mind was still in Dunlaoghaire waving at the two women standing on the deck of the boat. His head was still full of the excitement of his future with Annie.

As Sergeant Stone stopped on the platform for a few seconds to fix his hat on straight, out of the corner of his eye he saw the shadow of a gunman. Before he could react, he heard the shot and in almost the same instant he felt the bullet rip into his chest. He never felt the impact of the second bullet as he fell backwards from its impact. He was dead before his knees had time to buckle under his body weight. The gunman walked away in the opposite direction and out to the waiting Cab and Driver, the very same one that had brought the Sergeant, Annie and Carrie to the train earlier that same morning. As the gunman settled into the Cab he shouted out to the Driver, *"Well done, Whiskers, another blow for Irish freedom"*.

Sitting out on the deck of the boat and enjoying the fresh sea air Carrie Thompson and Annie Rogers were filled with excitement, they were heading out on a new adventure together. Annie still had butterflies in her stomach from the marriage proposal. Carrie stood up from her seat and facing Annie asked, *"Can I please be your Bridesmaid"?* Annie looked straight at her and replied, *"Of course you can, I was planning on asking you that when we reached Liverpool"*. Then Carrie, with a broad grin on her cheeky face, asked Annie, *"By the way, what's his name? Because we keeping calling him Sergeant Stone"* Annie looked at her and smiled *"Well now..."* she said *"...isn't that a good one, I never thought to ask him that question"*. The two of them laughed out loud together as Carrie's Pear-Drop earrings glistened in the sunshine.

An Accidental Murder

Business was slow and quiet for the two young women who stood under the gaze of a gas lamp situated on the corner of Elliott Place and Purdon Street. It was mid-week after all and most of the pubs in the area were almost empty at this time of night. Very few if any punters were likely to take up an offer of the girl's company and there weren't too many ships down by the Quayside either. But they stood there

51

nonetheless, living in hope, as a gentle haze of light rain enveloped them both.

Polly Spears, the eldest of the two young women, was a twenty-one-year-old from County Kilkenny. She had run away from an abusive home at thirteen years of age. On arriving in Dublin, she was soon befriended by an older girl who introduced her to a Madam from Railway Street. Polly shared her tenement room with her friend, Lizzie Hall, who stood next to her under the old street lamp. Lizzie was eighteen years of age, and as a new born baby she was abandoned by her mother who placed her gently down on a doorstep in Faithful Place and then walked away, never to return.

With the late night being cold and damp the two women decided to head off down the darkened street for a quiet drink before slipping home to bed. As they passed by the *"Man Trap"*, a small laneway situated at the back of the old pub, which was used on many occasions by Prostitutes and their male counterparts, to beat up and rob prospective customers, the two women noticed, what looked to them, to be a pile of old rags.

But on closer inspection they discovered the body of a young girl, aged about ten years old, fully dressed and lying on her back. Her pale young face was frozen in time with her two beautiful blue eyes wide open and staring up at the night sky. The young girl had a small raggy doll lying by her side. The two women stood in a state of shock horror at what they had discovered, unable to scream or shout for help, they stood with their hands over their mouths.

Suddenly and without warning, the back door of the pub opened wide and a shaft of light shone down on to the face of the young corpse. It was then that the two women screamed in frightened panic. The young barman, who had opened the door, quickly ran back inside to alert his father, the pub owner, as to what lay outside in the laneway. As the owner dashed out from behind the bar, he accidently knocked two empty drinking glasses off the counter.

His few customers who were sitting quietly sipping their drinks jumped with fright when the glasses smashed with a loud crash and their remains spread across the floor of the pub.

Three of the late-night drinkers jumped to their feet immediately and ran towards the back door, curious to know what the panic was all about. One of the three, Jimmy Price from White's Lane, on seeing the dead child, called out for the Police to be sent for. *"Ah Jaysus..."* he said *"...youse had better bring her in outta that rain, it wouldn't be a Christian thing to leave her out there, so it wouldn't"*. The Publican turned to his son and said *"Put your coat and cap on and get yourself up to the Police Station on Summerhill and be quick about it"*.

Soon enough the young bar tender arrived back on the scene with Police Sergeant Twomey and Constable PC32 from nearby Summerhill Police Station. The young victim had earlier been carried into the pub by the owner and one of his drinking pals and was laid out on a table next to the bar.

An older woman, Eliza Reilly, wrapped in a black shawl and sitting by the pub fire, put down her glass of Sherry and approached the dead child. *"Oh God have mercy on her poor soul..."* she gasped in fright, *"...sure that's young Molly Hayes from Railway Street"*. PC32, standing nearby with a pencil in one hand and a small black notebook in the other, began scribbling down all that was being said by the old woman. Sergeant Twomey, looking sternly at the woman asked, *"Are you sure about that Madam"? "Of course I am..."*, she replied, *"...sure isn't her father away at sea and her poor mother, God help her, is lying on her back in the Union Hospital"*. The Sergeant, turning to the young Constable said *"Get on over to Jervis Street Hospital as fast as you can and bring back some help to have this child taken away"*.

Polly Spears and Lizzie Hall, who had discovered the body, were seated by the pub fire, still crying and sipping a glass of whiskey each, compliments of the owner of the pub. Sergeant Twomey sat next to them, listening intently, as they related how it was that they happened to come upon the young child lying dead in the laneway. And like the young Constable earlier, he too had a pencil and note pad in his hands, writing down every word that came out of the mouths of the two young women.

News of the death of young Molly Hayes soon spread throughout the entire neighbourhood. No explanations were given as yet as to the cause of her death. But within an hour of her body being discovered rumours were rife all round that she was murdered by a Sailor and a foreign Sailor at that. Groups of men and women from the area took to the late-night streets in search of the *"Foreign Sailor"* but to no avail.

After the child was removed to the hospital and things had calmed down in the pub Sergeant Twomey made his way back to his Station up on Summerhill. He had more questions running around in his head than he had answers. Who could possibly have killed this young girl and why was there no blood on the body or at the scene where she was discovered? He would have to make contact with Dublin Castle and seek out their help in solving this mystery. Tomorrow would entail a visit to Jervis Street Hospital and a meeting with the main doctor in charge. The Sergeant knew there and then that he would not rest easy until such a time as he had solved this case.

The deceased, young ten-year-old Molly Hayes, it seems, was left to fend for herself from the very day that her mother was taken into hospital. She had no other family living nearby and her father, being away at sea, was out of all likely contact with home. The Parish Priest, Father Dowling, made the journey to the Union Hospital to inform Misses Hayes of the death of her only child and daughter, Molly.

Two young Constables came and questioned all of the neighbours living in the same tenement house as the Hayes family. The building was decrepit and ailing, a dark stairway enshrouded in the smells of unwashed bodies, boiled cabbage and rat droppings. Each door they knocked on was cautiously opened by those inside, with heads of unkempt scraggy hair, skeletal hands gripping the doors and dark eyes in shrunken faces staring out at the unwanted visitors, but nothing came of the policemen's efforts. Nobody it seems, had heard or seen anything out of the ordinary, nobody wanted to talk.

Molly had missed two days away from school. Her School Teacher, Miss Cassidy, put it down to Molly wanting to visit her mother in hospital and thought no more of it. Molly it seemed, was an unusually quiet girl who kept very much to herself, she was an only child who spent most of her time looking after her sick and ailing mother.

Sergeant Twomey was invited to Dublin Castle to present a case of murder to the Detective Unit based there. *"Gentlemen..."* he said, as he looked at the two Detectives seated in front of him. *"...I have it on good authority from the Hospital Pathologist that we are dealing with a possible case of murder"*. The two Detectives, Dixon and Gogarty, sat up in their chairs and asked *"And what is the cause of death Sergeant"? "It would appear that the child was smothered, sir..."* he replied, *"...that would explain why there was no sign of any blood on the victim. It seems, according to the Pathologist in Jervis Street Hospital, that the young girl possibly had a hand held over her mouth and that this may have caused her death. There was bruising found around the mouth and in no other area. Either way, I believe we are dealing with a murder".* "Righto Sergeant..." said Detective Dixon as he stood up from his chair, "...you keep on with your inquiries locally and if you need us, you know where we are". The Sergeant thanked the two Detectives and headed back to Summerhill.

Funeral arrangements were made for Molly's burial by the pub owner. A horse and cart were provided to carry her coffin to her place of burial. Her poor mother was unable to attend the funeral because of her medical condition. At the funeral Mass, Father Dowling, speaking from the Altar, urged anyone with information on Molly's death, to please speak to the Police or to himself, but he knew only too well that most people from this area of Dublin weren't too inclined to become involved with the Police, on any level. They would much prefer to make their own inquiries and deal out their own form of justice on the person or persons found guilty of Molly's murder.

One day turned to the next and still no sign of an arrest. Sergeant Twomey was more frustrated now than ever before, there had to be someone out there who either saw or heard something of this young girl's murder. The family's tenement room had been searched time and time again.

Nobody from the area or the tenement house was talking, not even Annie Taylor, who rented out the back parlour downstairs. Sergeant Twomey was convinced, none the less, that somebody out there knew something of what had happened to young Molly.

The Sergeant had two of his Constables walking up and down all of the nearby streets looking for any kind of a clue as to the murder but nothing showed up. They also spent time stopping people in the streets and asking for their help in trying to discover why young Molly Hayes had been murdered. Dublin Castle had lost interest in the case, they felt that they had more than enough to be doing with all the political agitation out on the streets.

Sometime after little Molly's funeral had taken place and as Sergeant Twomey was walking along Beaver Street doing his nightly rounds, he noticed a man kneeling down on the footpath ahead of him, seemingly to tie his shoe lace. As the Sergeant stepped around this figure, the man looked up and said, in a very quiet sort of way, *"I know who killed little Molly"*.

The Sergeant stood upright in surprise as he looked down at where the voice had come from. *"What's that you said?"* the Sergeant blurted out. The stranger, looking back up at him, replied in hushed tones, *"Be quiet man, for God's sake, not here. I'll tell you all later, we can't be seen talking together out here"*. When the Sergeant realised the seriousness of their situation he whispered, *"Don't leave it too late, you know where I'm at"*. He then headed off down towards Foley Street, more puzzled than ever before and made his way back to the Station on Summerhill. The stranger stood up and walked away in the opposite direction, heading off into the darkness of the night, now and then, throwing a cautious glance over his shoulder out of fear of being followed.

In the back parlour of number twenty Railway Street, next door to O'Reilly's Pawn Shop, were four men, Charlie Smithers, Joxer McCabe, Jimmy Doyle and Tommy Butler, also present was a young woman named Annie Taylor, a twenty-six-year-old *"Lady of the Night"*. They all sat around a table speaking in low whispers to each other. *"So..."* said the woman as she leaned into the group, *"...and where do we go from here, now that everything has quietened down, at last"*?

The men all looked cautiously around at each other for an answer to her question. *"Where indeed..."* answered Charlie Smithers as he stubbed out a cigarette butt onto the top surface of the old table. He was just as unsure about their situation as the rest of the group. *"…we can't just sit around twiddling our thumbs now, can we"*?

Jimmy Doyle stood up, shuffled around the room and with all heads turning in his direction, he eventually leaned across the table and said, *"Now, as far as we know, that money is still in that Pawn Shop and we need to get in there and help ourselves to it. What's happened has happened, it was an accident and as far as I'm concerned, none of us is to blame"*.

The robbery had gone belly-up soon after it had begun. Their plan was to break in through the back wall next to the tenement house and gain access to the Pawn Shop situated next door. The gang leader, Willie Smithers, had been tipped off a few days earlier by a young boy, an employee of the Pawn Broker, that a large amount of money was being stored in the wall safe of the premises. Smithers reckoned that if his gang could break through the wall from the outside yard of the shop then they could gain access to the Safe and the money.

Annie Taylor's part in the plan was to have her stand outside the front door of the tenement house on Railway Street and pretend to be *"On the Game"* for any men passing by but in fact, her part in the robbery was to keep an eye out for any *"Rozzers"*, a name locally given to policemen, who might be passing up or down the street. One of the men would stand at the back entrance to the tenement hallway and if Annie whistled, then he was to alert the rest of the men to the presence of the Rozzers. They would immediately stop their hammering and banging and sit down on the ground as quiet as mice, not stirring an inch, until Annie gave a second whistle for the *"All Clear"*, indicating that the Rozzers had gone on their way and enabling the gang to continue with the break in. They would then carry off the Safe and the money.

At the commencement of the robbery Molly Hayes was sitting quietly at the end of her mother's bed and holding her doll on her lap. It was a doll that her father had brought home for her from some strange naming place he had visited overseas. Sometimes she would cuddle up to the doll at night while her father was away at sea and pretend to talk to him in her dreams. Molly felt that she had no worries where her mother was concerned because of the lovely Nurses that were taking care of her in the Union Hospital.

Suddenly and out of nowhere, Molly heard a great big banging and thumping noise coming from the backyard down below the window of her room which was situated at the top of the tenement house. The noise didn't scare or upset her at all because there was always some banging, shouting or crying going on most nights in the house. The banging was just unusual at this late hour.

As the gang of robbers were preparing to begin their work, Tommy Butler was assigned to stand at the back entrance to the hallway of the tenement house and keep an ear out for Annie Taylor's whistle of warning. He stood in a dark corner of the hallway so as to be invisible to anyone passing by.

Tommy was a small nervous type of man, continuously smoking and coughing and always looking over his shoulder. For a man of his size, he had unusually big hands, he had often worked down on the Dockside unloading cargos of wheat from Canada and shovelling coal from boats that had arrived over from England. On this particular night however, he stood tense and nervous, he had only agreed to help the gang out at the last minute because work was slow in coming his way.

Back upstairs, young Molly had decided to fetch a bucket of water from the tap located in the backyard down below, she wanted to make herself a cup of cocoa before going to sleep for the night and she needed the water to boil the kettle.

Molly made her way slowly but surely down the dark stairs from her room, holding the bucket in one hand and her raggy doll in the other while walking with her back to the wall to avoid stepping on any rats or mice that may be about. That was how her mother told her to go down the stairs in the dark, slowly and carefully.

As she reached the bottom of the stairs Molly saw a woman standing outside the open door of the house, leaning against the old iron rail, in the rain. The woman didn't pay any attention to Molly. And so, she walked out along the hall, swinging the bucket as she went down the two or three steps that led out into the yard, unaware of the figure hiding in the dark recess of the hallway, watching her every move as she passed by.

Molly could still hear the banging noises that she had heard from her room up above, but only now, they were louder than ever before. She walked over to the water tap, placed her bucket on the ground below it and turned it on. As the water was filling the bucket Molly decided to go and see what all the banging was about. Her curiosity had gotten the better of her.

Annie Taylor, in the meantime, was on full alert as she looked up and down the street in the rain-washed darkness of the night. The street was long and empty with not a sinner in sight. There was an echo of crying babies in the air and the shouting of voices and the banging of doors. It was then that Annie suddenly spotted two tall figures appearing almost out of nowhere near the corner of Faithful Place and Railway Street and they were heading her way too. Quickly recognising them in their police uniforms, Annie turned her head and gave a sharp whistle into the hallway of the tenement house.

Tommy Butler quickly sprang out of his place of hiding and on running out to the backyard to warn his friends, he spotted the small figure of Molly Hayes. Molly had become more curious about all the banging as she walked towards the broken wall that divided the two back yards, clutching her little doll. She had no idea what was going on or what was about to happen. In a blind panic, Tommy Butler alerted his companions in crime to the warning whistle from Annie Taylor and at the same time wrapped one of his great big hands over the mouth of young Molly Hayes to prevent her from screaming with fright at his sudden appearance and thus perhaps, alerting the police to his presence.

One of the policemen, on approaching Annie Taylor, took a cigarette out of his pocket and offered it to her, the other policeman struck a match. Annie pretended to be grateful to the two of them. They stood, one each side of her, and engaged her in conversation. The talk was casual at first and then they asked her about the men she was hoping to do business with and if she knew of any criminal activity taking place in the area. They stood talking to Annie for the best part of ten minutes and all this time little Molly Hayes was fighting and scratching in blind panic at the great big hand that covered her mouth and prevented her from breathing.

And in a likewise state of panic, Tommy Butler placed more pressure on the hand over Molly's mouth, he knew that he could not afford to let her scream, he had no intention of ending up in prison. When the time came for the two policemen to continue on their beat, Molly Hayes had stopped fighting and wriggling under the tight grip of Tommy Butler's hand. When he finally removed it from Molly's mouth, her little knees buckled and she dropped to the ground, poor young Molly lay there lifeless and still, she was dead.

At that very moment, Tommy Butler was unaware of Molly's condition as he looked down at her, he was convinced that she had just fainted, or had she? For a split second he questioned himself. It was then however, that he heard another whistle from Annie Taylor, letting him know that the coast was clear and for him to inform his friends to continue with their work.

On his return to his hideaway in the hallway and as Tommy stepped over Molly, he noticed that the water tap was still turned on and that the bucket was overflowing. He walked over, turned off the tap, picked up the heavy bucket and made his way back over to where Molly was lying on the ground. He nudged her with his foot once or twice in an effort to wake her up but with no success. Once again, he tried the same tactic but again with no success. Tommy laid the bucket down on the ground close to Molly and kneeling beside her, next to the little doll, he shook her little form before turning her over onto her back.

Even now, as he stared up close at her, Tommy was quite unsure of Molly's condition but at the back of his mind there was some little question of doubt and so he ran out along the hallway to Annie Taylor. *"Quick Annie..."* he said to her with panic written all over his face. *"...I think something has happened to the Young One"*. Annie turned her head to look at him and seeing the panic in his eyes asked him, *"What Young One are you talking about Tommy"?* He stuttered and stammered in his attempt to reply to her question. *"The little one on the ground out in the backyard, the little one on the ground, I think she's dead".* Annie quickly looked up and down the street and seeing no one about turned and ran with Tommy along the length of the hallway.

It didn't take Annie long to realise that the young child lying on the ground at her feet was indeed dead. Leaving Tommy staring down at the little one, Annie ran into the yard next door to inform the rest of their gang about the lifeless child and warned them to call off their plans to rob the Pawn Shop. Tommy came up behind Annie and looking at his companions blurted out *"I did it, I killed her, but I didn't mean to, I swear I didn't. I couldn't let her scream or we would have all been caught and sent to Jail".* The men all looked back and forward at each other, they couldn't believe what they were hearing, this just couldn't be happening.

Without another word being said and with a nod from Charlie Smithers, everyone quickly and quietly took up their tools and walked silently away from the rear of the Pawn Shop. As they each passed by poor little Molly they stopped and looked down at her. Charlie Smithers told Jimmy Doyle to pick up the young girl and her doll and to carry them both inside to their back room next door in number twenty. They all shuffled off into their room and sat there in complete silence, each stunned by the death of the young child. Jimmy Doyle laid poor Molly down on the table in the centre of the room.

"So, what now..." said Annie Taylor, with a furious look on her face as she stared across the room at Tommy Butler, *"...what do we do now is what I want to know"*. Butler was crying as he placed his bent head in his hands and said *"I didn't mean to kill the child but I couldn't take the chance in case she screamed, I'm so sorry it happened, I'm so sorry"*. Charlie Smithers stood up with a serious look on his face and looking around at each one in the room, said in a quiet whisper, *"We'll just have to get rid of her so, won't we? Nobody saw or heard anything and nobody will talk even if they did"*. Everyone nodded in agreement. *"And the sooner the better we do it"* replied Annie Taylor.

Once the body of Molly Hayes was quietly stowed away in the lane behind the pub, the gang once again returned to their tenement room and gathered around the table in silence. They had all agreed earlier that the *"Man Trap"* was considered as good a place as any under the circumstances because it was mainly used at night by prostitutes, other people from the area rarely if ever ventured into it, even during daytime. This would hopefully give the gang enough time to think of ways to cover themselves in case any of them were hauled in by the Police for questioning.

Neither one of them went home or slept that night. Jimmy Doyle was talking to himself about making plans to escape across the Irish Sea to England and his brother who lived somewhere in Manchester. Annie Taylor was planning on taking the earliest train she could catch to Belfast, where her sister still lived in the family home. Everyone else sat quietly around the table, unsure of what to say or do. Joxer McCabe blurted out that if they all kept their traps shut and said nothing to no one, then they'd all be as safe as houses because no one would know anything about what had happened.

The following day after the encounter by Sergeant Twomey and the shoe lace stranger, a young boy arrived at the police station and asked to see the Sergeant. It just so happened that the Sergeant was standing next to the Constable who was on counter duty when the boy arrived. *"And what would you be wanting with me"?* said the Sergeant as he looked down over the counter at the young boy.

The boy looked up at the two faces staring down at him

and in a frightened voice replied, *"Eh, a man gave me a penny to bring this piece of paper in here and to give it to youse"* said the boy as he reached up his hand to the Sergeant. *"And what was the man's name"*? asked the Sergeant. *"Eh I don't know sir, he never told me"*, replied the young boy. The Sergeant took a quick look at the note and then reaching in under the counter took out a sweet lollipop and handed it down to the boy. *"Well done, you're a good lad. Now be on your way"* he said. The boy grabbed the lollipop and was gone out the door of the station as quickly as he had come in.

The Sergeant sat down at his desk and slowly read the contents of the note that the young boy had handed up to him. It asked that he, the Sergeant, dress in civilian clothes and make his way to a particular pub on the south side of the city, well away from the prying eyes of the area where young Molly Hayes was discovered and that he come no later than seven o'clock that very same evening. There was no name or signature on the note.

It was some days after the attempted robbery and the demise of poor little Molly Hayes, when Tommy Butler came tumbling drunk up the stairway of the tenement house where he lived on the second floor. One of his neighbours from the third floor, Billy Caulfield, was coming down the stairs when he saw Tommy and noticing the state he was in, attempted to help him into his room.

The neighbour was an old pal who had often worked alongside Tommy down on the Docks. He was surprised however, to see Tommy this drunk so early in the day, this was just not like him at all. Because of the state of Tommy his neighbour decided to stay with him in case he had received some bad news or other. He helped Tommy up on to his bed and removed his shoes for him. Tommy lay there crying and mumbling into his pillow. *"I didn't mean it, honest to God, I didn't mean it"*. His neighbour became even more puzzled than before. And then it happened.

Billy Caulfield placed a kind and tender hand on Tommy's shoulder and said *"Now, don't be fretting Tommy, it can't be all that bad. Do you want to tell me what's going on for yeah"*? Tommy slowly turned his head around and glared at his friend, with his eyes almost jumping out of his head, *"It was an accident I tell yeah..."* he growled, *"...an accident, I didn't mean for the child to die so I didn't"*.

Billy was even more puzzled and afraid now than ever before. He sat down on the side of the bed and giving Tommy a good shake, he asked, *"For the love of God*

Tommy, what child are you talking about"?

Tommy slowly sat upright and giving his friend a most frightful look, said, *"It was me; it was me who killed that little girl, Molly Hayes, now do you know"?* Still unsure of what he was hearing, Billy said in reply, *"Are you out of your mind man, sure you wouldn't hurt a fly never mind kill a child. Do you know what you are saying for God's sake"?* Tommy moved his face nearer to that of his neighbour. *"Amn't I after tellin' yeah? Sure, the Priest won't even come to me funeral. They'll be after putting a rope around me neck and I'll go to Hell for sure".* Tommy began to shiver and shake at the very thought of what might lay ahead of him.

Billy looked around the room and seeing a teapot sitting by the fire grate walked over to see if there was any liquid inside. *"Now..."* he said across the room to Tommy, *"...I'll heat us up a mug of tea each and you can tell me all about it. It's probably not as bad as you think".*

Sergeant Twomey arrived at his destination with a few minutes to spare. As he stepped inside the pub door, he gave a quick glance around the room with his well-trained Policeman's Eye. It was unusually quiet for a pub and there were no more than half a dozen customers drinking at the Bar. Over in one corner of the room however he quickly spotted the *"Shoe Lace"* man sitting on his own. Having being given the nod the Sergeant ordered himself a pint of Stout and with the drink in his hand he made his way across the bar-room floor towards his would-be informant.

For the first few minutes or so the two men sat together in total silence. The Sergeant knew the face well but not the name of Billy Caulfield. Having taken a couple of sips from his drink the Sergeant leaned his head in close to his informer and said, *"Well, what have you to tell me about Molly Hayes then"?* Billy gave a quick and cautious glance around the room before answering. And then, pretending to take a sip from his own glass and while holding it up close to his mouth said to the Sergeant in a low whisper, *"It was an accident, she wasn't supposed to die, he didn't mean to kill her you know and anyway she shouldn't have been down there at that late hour of the night."* The Sergeant was taken aback by what he was hearing and for a moment he was even in doubt as to what was being said.

Slowly lifting up his glass, the Sergeant took a sip of its contents to give himself a moment or two to let everything he'd heard so far sink in. He then turned to his informer and said in a very forceful but low voice, *"Now, I think you had better tell me the whole story and I mean everything or I'll* have to drag you over to the Station and have it beaten out of you, the choice is yours". Billy Caulfield knew well that if he refused to do what the Sergeant said he was in deep trouble. He looked around the room once again and glancing at the Sergeant, he said, "Not here, it's too open and there's too much to tell, we'll have to go elsewhere". "Okay so..." said the Sergeant, "...we'll slip in around the corner to Kevin Street Station, nobody will know you there. Now, drink up and let's go".

Charlie Smithers and Annie Taylor were sitting together by the fire in the semi darkness of number 20 Railway Street. The rest of their gang had long gone home. Charlie had asked Annie to delay her departure to Belfast for a few days because he had something to put to her about the night of the robbery and its possible consequences. "Well..." said Annie as she sat there with a cigarette sticking out of the side of her mouth, "...what do you want to talk to me about, what's on your mind"?

Charlie was sitting uneasy on his chair by the fire and fidgeting with the cap in his hand, unsure as to how or where to start this conversation. "Well, you see...', he hesitated for a moment or two and then continued on when he felt a little more composed, "...I think we're all in danger of being *shopped to the Police and I think I know who it is that might drop us right in it"*. Annie turned more towards him with a surprised look on her face. *"What do you mean by that..."* she said to him, *"...are you trying to tell me that one of the lads might spill the beans on us"?* Charlie lifted his head slightly and with a little grin on his unshaven face he answered her. *"That's exactly what I'm saying and I think I know who it might be as well".*

With fright, Annie dropped the cup of tea she had in her hand and let it crash to the floor. *"You must be outta your head, none of the lads would dare utter a word to anyone and especially to the Rozzers..."*, she uttered. Willie continued to stare at her with that *"Know-it-all"* smirk still on his face. *"...so, tell me then, who do you think it is"?* she said back at him through gritted teeth, not wanting to believe what he was about to suggest. *"I think Tommy Butler could possibly drop us all in it. I don't believe he can hold it together. He was crying at the child's funeral for God's sake and everyone looking at him, wondering what was going on".*

Annie couldn't believe what she was hearing. Her face dropped, she could see the strong possibility of people from the area, who had attended the funeral, putting two and two together and heading up to Summerhill for some kind of reward for their information. She looked intently at Smithers and said, "A*nd* what *do you intend to do about it may I ask"?* Smithers looked straight back at her and replied, *"Do you mean, what are "We" going to do about it"?*

Sergeant Twomey had arranged for a Constable to sit in the interview room with him, to take notes of what was being said and to witness the telling of the story, while he himself listened intently to every word his informer had to say about the murder of Molly Hayes. The Informer had made sure to include every last detail as told to him by Jimmy Butler, including a list of names of those involved in the attempted robbery on the night that Molly Hayes died and also the name of Annie Taylor. One and a half hours later the room fell into silence, the telling of the story had finally come to an end.

The Sergeant stood up and nodded to his informant to do the same. He looked across the room at the Constable, thanked him for his time and reminded him to be careful when typing up the conversation that had just taken place and to make doubly sure that nothing was left out. The Constable reassured the Sergeant that he would follow his instructions to the letter and he would ensure that a copy of the statement would find its way to Detective Dixon in Dublin Castle the next day. The Sergeant and his informer left the Police Station, he thanked him for all he had told, they then shook hands and parted ways.

Charlie Smithers and Annie Taylor had both agreed on a plan to shut Tommy Butler up, permanently. *"Right so..."* said Annie, looking up at the taller Smithers, *"...we'll both make our way up to his room together and take care of business, is that the plan"*? *"You have it in one..."* he replied. *"...you get him to lay down on the bed and when he falls to sleep, I'll put a pillow over his face and finish him off, he'll die the same way as the young girl died. Now..."* he reminded her, *"... be sure to fill him up with drink first, that way it'll look like he died in his sleep"*.

Very late that night and heading into the early hours of the next morning Smithers and Taylor made their way silently up the darkened stairway of Tommy Butler's tenement house to the second landing and knocked ever so gently on his door. The last thing they needed were nosey neighbours hearing anything or knowing of their presence there. Opening his door and looking inside, they found Tommy stripped to the waist and sitting by the fire with a cigarette sticking out from the side of his mouth. In the semi darkness of the room, he looked like a tormented man about to be led to the gallows.

Annie was the first one to approach him. *"Ah Tommy, me oul darling..."* she said in a false caring sort of way. *"...we heard you weren't well and thought we'd call in and see if we could cheer you up"*. Charlie Smithers moved closer to Tommy and placing a hand on his arm said, *"Sure there you are now Tommy, me oul pal, don't you be worrying about anything, sure we'll soon have that money outta the Pawn Shop and then we'll all be smiling"*.

Annie held a large bottle of whiskey up in front of Tommy's face. *"Look what Charlie brought up for yeah, sure this'll warm the cockles of your heart and have you as right as rain in next to no time at all"*. Tommy never moved an inch from the time the pair came into his room as he sat staring into the dying embers of the fire. With a nudge from Smithers, Annie lifted Tommy up onto his feet and walking him towards the bed, took the cigarette out of his mouth and began to smoke it herself. *"Come on now me little darling..."* she said as she coaxed him towards the bed, *"...sure you and meself will lay down on the bed together for a bit of comfort"*.

Smithers gave Annie another nudge and pointed with his head at the bottle of whiskey. Annie had a quick change of mind and had Butler sit down on the edge of his bed. *"Now, sit there a minute me oul pet and we'll have Willie open up this bottle for us, sure we can't be going to bed thirsty, now that wouldn't do at all"*. Still, there was no reaction from Tommy to the presence of either one of his visitors.

Annie held the open bottle up to Tommy's mouth, almost choking him as she poured more than enough of the whiskey down his throat. He spluttered and coughed and gasped for breath. In next to no time at all the drink was having an effect on him. He was murmuring and crying with his head resting gently on Annie's bosom. Pouring more drink into him, she laid Tommy down upon the bed and began singing softly into his ear.

With his eyes soon closed, Tommy had fallen into a deep drunken sleep. Charlie Smithers gently removed the pillow from under Tommy's head and placed it over his face, pressing down on it with all his strength and might. As Tommy was struggling for breath and thrashing about, Annie climbed out of the bed and she too began to press down on the pillow. After a couple of minutes Tommy lay still and quiet, no movement out of him.

The other two stood side by side next to the bed, looking down at poor Tommy and both with grins of satisfaction painted across their evil faces. Annie turned and facing Charlie, she threw her arms around his neck and kissed him on the lips. Leaving the pillow lying across poor Tommy's face, Charlie threw his two arms around Molly's waist. Soon enough however, the two of them, ever so quietly, made their way out of the tenement house and disappeared into the darkness of the rain-soaked night.

Because Tommy Butler was the quiet sort of individual he was, his absence from anywhere in particular would never have caused alarm to his neighbours or friends because he was sure to turn up at some stage of the day or other.

However, Mary Fitzers, his neighbour from across the hall, who was heading out to Mass, noticed that the door to Tommy's room was slightly open and thinking that maybe he had gone out and forgotten to close it properly or that, she went to shut it for him. But for some reason or other, which Mary was later unable to explain to the priest, the police or to her neighbours, she felt something was just not right about the door being left opened. She ever so quietly peeped into the room and as her eyes adjusted to the semi darkness, she saw what looked like Tommy lying on the bed, with a pillow over his face.

It seems that, Charlie Smithers and Annie Taylor, had become so caught up in their hugging and kissing after smothering Tommy, that they had forgotten to remove the pillow from off of his face before they left his room. They were also too busy gulping down the remaining whiskey from the bottle that Annie still held in her hand. Mary Fitzers screams soon brought all of the neighbours in the tenement house running up and down the stairway to the scene of the crime. As some of the neighbours tried to calm Mary down a young lad and his sister were sent off to fetch the Police.

Sergeant Twomey soon arrived at the tenement flat with two of his Constables in tow. The neighbours were all asked to leave the room with the exception of Mary Fitzers and her pal, Bessy McGrath, who busied herself making a cup of tea for Mary, to help steady her nerves. The Sergeant soon realised that Tommy's death and that of little Molly Hayes were in some way connected, this was not, in his own way of thinking, an accidental murder.

He had earlier arranged with the owner of the Pawn Shop to move the large amount of money from his safe up to the Police Station, without telling anyone working for him or otherwise, of the arrangement. The Sergeant wanted the gang to believe that the money was still in the safe, as he was sure they would try again to break in from the backyard. Two days later one of the Constables from the Station, reported to the Sergeant that he had received a tip-off that the gang were indeed going to attempt another break-in to the Pawnshop and that it was to take place in the late hours of that very night. The Sergeant made immediate contact with the Detective Unit in Dublin Castle and spoke to them about the second murder. They had already received a copy of his report on the murder interview that the Sergeant had carried out earlier with his informant, Billy Caulfield and would arrive armed and ready for action.

Later that evening a meeting was called for in the Station to inform everyone of what plan was being put into place for later that night. The Sergeant had a firearm firmly placed in a holster by his side. He had arranged for twenty extra men to be brought into the area to help with arresting and containing all of those involved with the attempted Pawn Shop robbery and the murder of Molly Hayes.

Detective Dixon stood up and addressed the large group of Police Constables and Detectives who were seated and standing around in the Station. He made it quite clear that no action was to be taken without his say so. He pointed to his companion, Detective Gogarty, who stood up and reminded all those present that were armed to hold their fire and not to shoot unless someone's life was in danger. He gave a purposeful glance across the room at Sergeant Twomey, knowing only too well, that if given half a chance, he intended to sort out the brutes involved in the robbery of the Pawn Shop and the murder of Molly Hayes, with the aid of his weapon.

It was shortly after midnight when Charlie Smithers and his gang returned to the scene of their proposed robbery. Because they were short of one man compared to the last time they were here, Annie Taylor would have to play a double role tonight. She was told to keep an eye out on the street for any patrolling policemen and to run through the hallway of the tenement house to warn the gang of their coming, her whistling was of no use to her this time.

The gang members all brought out their tools from the back parlour room and crossed over into the yard at the rear of the Pawn Shop. Soon enough the hammering and banging commenced, the loud noises shattering the stillness of the night as most families in the tenement house next door were settling down to sleep.

Annie stood outside the doorway of the tenement house, nervous and afraid this time in hope that nothing would go wrong with the robbery. All she wanted was her share of the money and a train ticket back to Belfast. Most of the men out back, hammering and banging, were of a similar frame of mind to Annie, all they wanted was their fair share of the money and a ticket out of town.

The barking of a dog further down Railway Street broke the stillness of the night and attracted Annie's attention in that direction. At first, she was unsure as to what exactly it was she was looking at. In the semi darkness of the night, it looked like a large group of men who were drunk. Then, as they passed under a street lamp, Annie caught sight of uniforms, it was the Police, at least ten or twelve of them, and they were running down the street in her direction. She took to her heels and ran out along the hallway towards the back yard, losing one of her shoes in panic. She began shouting out a warning and calling for Charlie Smithers to make a run for it. With the noise of all the hammering and banging going on nobody was able to hear what Annie was saying. But Charlie Smithers could tell by the frightened look on her face that all was not well.

He took to his heels and headed out towards the tenement hallway with Annie running after him, he never bothered to warn the rest of his men to the possibility of a police presence. As the two of them ran up the two or three steps leading from the backyard into the hallway they came to a sudden stop.

Standing there in front of them and blocking any chance of escape out onto the street, were the group of policemen that Annie had seen earlier. Smithers mind went into a blind panic, what was he to do? Then, suddenly and without warning, Sergeant Twomey and his two detective friends stepped out of the shadow of the darkened recess where Tommy Butler had hidden on the night of Molly Hayes's death, each of them armed and pointing their guns at Smithers and Taylor.

In a rapid and quick move Smithers grabbed Annie Taylor around the neck, and placing her in front of him like a shield, he drew out a gun from inside his trouser band and held it to her head. Annie was screaming at him to put the gun down but he just kept staring at Sergeant Twomey. *"Okay..."* said Smithers to the Sergeant, *"...you lot put your weapons down on the ground and stand back out of my way or she'll get it in the head. So, don't get any smart ideas like trying to follow me or it'll be her corpse you'll be picking up off the street"*.

As Annie tried to turn around to plead with Smithers for her life, she pushed against him and knocked him off balance, causing him to sway on his feet. Then suddenly and without warning, Smithers gun let off a shot that echoed throughout the hallway, taking everyone by surprise. Annie let out a scream as she fell to the floor, she was shot in the back. The two Detectives immediately fired a shot each into Smithers. He fell back against the wall while still gripping the gun in his hand.

Sergeant Twomey slowly raised his own weapon and taking careful aim, shot Charlie Smithers straight in the forehead, one very clean shot right between his two eyes, finally ending it all. Everyone stood in stunned silence as Smither fell to the floor. The Sergeant lowered his gun as the echo of the shot reverberated up throughout the entire house.

The Sergeant looked over his shoulder at the group of shocked and frightened young policemen gathered around the door of the house and catching the attention of PC32 said *"Didn't you see him raise that gun with the intention of putting our lives in danger"?* The young constable stood for a few seconds with his mouth open and then replied, more in fear of the Sergeant than anything else, *"Yes, Sergeant, I did indeed, that's exactly what I saw"*. The Sergeant glared at the two detectives standing beside him, almost daring them to say anything different and said *"Well let that be the end of it so"*.

PC 32 shouted out an order to his fellow policemen to arrest the rest of the gang out back and to make it snappy. Up on the first landing of the tenement house a group of neighbours stood watching and listening at the policemen below. The Sergeant, looking up at them as he placed his gun back in its holster, shouted up at them, *"Now, ladies and gentlemen, the show is over. Off to bed with you all."*

And so, they all shuffled off to their rooms. Sergeant Twomey and the two Detectives walked side by side out of the hallway and into the freshness of the cold night air. Sergeant Twomey turned to them both and shaking their hands said *"And a good night to you both"*. He then turned around and headed back to his Station up on Summerhill.

Finnegan's Pub

I will never forget that winters night and the sound of the gunshot. I was less than two feet away from the gunman and his victim, Jemmy O'Hare. I was no more than twelve years old at the time and Jemmy was probably in his mid-thirties and single. I was going around the pub collecting up any empty beer glasses that were on the tables, that was one of the jobs I used to do for Mister Finnegan who owned the pub. The place was quite full with everyone huddled together as they sat in out of the cold of the night. All of a sudden and without warning, two tall men came into the pub, a third man held the door open to accommodate his comrades proposed quick escape.

They each wore a dark coloured Gabardine Coat, tied tightly around their waist with a belt and each had their collars pulled up. Each of them wore a Trilby Hat pulled down over their eyes. I remember everyone looking around in surprise at them because they looked like gangsters out of a film and with the pub door open there was an awful cold draft coming in. *"Here..."* someone shouted out, *"...shut that door after yeah"*.

Without saying a word or acknowledging the complaining drinkers, the two men walked straight up to Jemmy O'Hare, who was standing at the bar with his back to them. The barman, young Joe Finnegan, said something to Jemmy, who turned to face the two strange men. As soon as eye contact was made one of the men spoke out over the hushed silence of the drinkers, *"Are you James O'Hare"?* he asked in what I remember as a country accent. Jemmy slowly put his pint down on the counter, stood erect and facing the two men replied in a very stern and threatening voice, *"What if*

I am and what's it to you anyway"? The second man pulled a gun out of his pocket and pointing it at Jemmy, pulled the trigger and shot a bullet into his chest.

To me, and maybe because I was so near to the action, it all seemed to happen in slow-motion from the moment the gun appeared on the scene. The boom from the explosion of the gunshot enveloped me totally and all other sounds ceased to exist, I could hear nothing but the resounding ringing of bells locked inside my little head. The two men made a swift and rapid exit and as they did the gunman almost tripped over me, I didn't realise that I was standing in his way, he looked down at me with a scowl on his face and was gone.

I knew everyone in the pub was screaming and shouting but I could only hear the bells inside my head. The force of the bullet entering Jemmy's chest threw him backwards and he fell over a table onto the floor. Mister Lawlor and his brother-in-law, Mister Quinn had been sitting at that table and they too were knocked to the floor with Jemmy landing on top of them.

Mister Quinn, who was still holding his beer glass, began to roar and shout, *"Ah Mother of Divine Mercy, would someone take this fella up off me"*. But no one seemed to pay him any attention as most of the men in the pub made a very quick and panicked exit when they realised what had happened. They didn't want to get involved. The women in the Snug were roaring and screaming in to their husbands telling them to get out of there quick. It was then that I dropped the four glasses I was carrying and began screaming as they smashed across the floor.

Mister Finnegan came running out from behind the bar and lifted me up in his arms. Holding me in a tight grip around my waist he brought me out to the back hall and up the stairs to my mother. We lived in the rooms up over the pub, myself, my widowed mother and my two younger sisters, Anne and Mary. My father had died the year before in an accident while unloading a ship down on the Docks.

He had been great friends with Mister Finnegan and after his funeral my mother was offered two rooms up over the pub, free of rent, all she had to do in return was to clean around the place, do a bit of cooking and let me help out whenever I was needed. We had our own toilet and running water in this flat and real electricity.

Sometimes I would help young Joe Finnegan down in the basement with bottling the Stout and he'd show me how to use the gadget for corking the bottles when they were filled.

Most days after school I would go out around the tenement houses and the brothels and side streets collecting any empty Stout Bottles that had been sold from the pub over the past few days. I would have to wash them out and have them ready for re-filling. I also kept the cellar clean and tidy. Myself and my two sisters loved living here because before that we lived in a room in a tenement house at the far end of Waterford Street, it was full of rats and it smelled.

When my mother had heard the gunshot, she came running down the stairs with her hands in the air and screaming out at the top of her voice, *"Oh Holy Mary and Sweet Jesus Divine, don't let anything happen to my son"*. When she saw me in Mister Finnegan's arms, she burst out crying. *"I'm alright Ma'..."* I said to her *"...they didn't shoot me"*.

My hearing was beginning to return back to normal. Mister Finnegan continued carrying me up to our room and in between tears, my mother was asking him what had happened. *"Well now..."* said Mister Finnegan as he put me sitting down on the edge of my mother's bed, *"...you and I saw nothing, we heard nothing and so, we'll say nothing"*. He then looked down at me and winked. I knew straightaway that I too was expected to pay attention to that little bit of King Solomon's Wisdom that he had shared with my mother. And so, I too kept my mouth shut, as best I could that is.

The whole pub was unusually quiet and almost empty after the shooting. Misses Mac was standing beside the pub counter where poor old Jemmy was laid out and she was reciting a decade of the Rosary over him. Her pal, Misses Downes was blessing Jemmy from a bottle of Lourdes Holy Water that she always carried in her apron pocket.

Mister and Misses McDermot from Faithful Place had run over to the Pro Cathedral for a Priest. Before they arrived back however, two Detectives from Dublin Castle and three Dublin Metropolitan Policemen came into the pub. The first thing they did was to put the run on the two women who were praying over poor Jemmy.

Upstairs, my mother had told the three of us to get into her bed and stay as quite as a mouse so that she could hear what was going on down below. You see, out in the small hallway upstairs, Mister Finnegan had made a hole in the floor that went down through the ceiling into the pub, so that he could keep an eye on things from upstairs without too many people knowing. It also gave him the advantage of being able to pick up on certain conversations going on at the bar.

He had put two paint marks on the counter directly below where the hole was, most of the locals knew that they weren't to stand in between these two marks, it was to be reserved for any strangers who came into the pub and when they stood there, Mister Finnegan could go upstairs and listen in on their conversation and in that way, he would know what they were about and might even pick up some valuable information for *'Special friends'* of his.

This is where my mother had her ear pinned to while she was earwigging on what the Police were saying. What she wasn't aware of was that us three younger ones had sneaked out of our beds and were standing right behind her trying to listen in as well. Mister Finnegan and his son, young Joe, as everyone called him, were standing in behind the bar.

The three policemen were standing guard around the pub while one of the detectives was writing something down in a notebook. The other detective leaned across the counter and resting himself on the corpse said, *"Now, Mister Finnegan, what's this body doing on your counter and who put it there"*?

Mister Finnegan was a widower, sometime after his wife died, he bought over the pub. He was originally from County Wexford and used to tell stories across the bar, to anyone that would listen that is, about his grandfather who fought in the Battle of Vinegar Hill during the Wexford Rising of 1798. Mister Finnegan pulled himself up to his six feet in height and looking the detective straight in the eye, replied, *"To tell you the truth now Officer, I have no idea how that corpse got there or who put it there, me and my son here were taking a young boy upstairs to safety after the shot rang out and that's the truth of it. We know nothing other than that"*. At the end of this statement, he eye-balled his son.

The Detective then turned to young Joe and said, *"And what did you see before the shooting"?* Young Joe looked at his father again for reassurance. *"Well, go on young Joe, tell the man what you know"*, said his father. As I was later to discover, the tone to this order from the older man was a well-rehearsed piece of dialogue between father and son, they had definitely done this before. *"You see sir..."* said a very nervous young Joe, *"...I was down in the basement bringing up a few crates of stout when I heard the shot but I didn't know what it was and I had to help me father with the young fella going upstairs"*. *"There now, that's grand..."* said his father, *"...go off to bed with you and give your nerves a rest, we can talk about this in the morning"*.

Young Joe did as he was told, much to the annoyance of the two detectives. However, instead of going into the back room to his bed, he came up the stairs and joined my mother at the Peep-Hole. We younger ones continued to stand around trying to catch the gist of the conversation going on down below.

Mister Finnegan stood with his arms folded across his chest, in defiance of the detective's questions. It was at this point that Mister and Misses McDermot arrived back with the Priest in tow. Father O'Sullivan was the first to burst in through the door of the pub and he was furious, brushing past the Policeman on door duty, he shouted out in a good old Kenmare accent, *"Now, Mister Finnegan this had better be good, I don't appreciate being dragged out of my bed at this late hour, I'm telling you that now"*.

He walked straight into the Detective with the notebook. The priest took one glance at him and tried to push past but the Detective stood his ground. *"What in blazes is going on here and who are you may I ask"* said the very impatient Father O'Sullivan. *"I am Detective Sergeant Mulligan and this here is Detective Inspector Rogers, we're here from Dublin Castle"*.

The priest stood still and looking around the pub, noticed poor Jemmy lying on the counter with his chest all covered in blood. *"Is he drunk or is he dead"?* asked the priest in a very sarcastic manner. Without waiting for an answer, he proceeded to give the dead man the Last Rites and then left the pub as quickly as he had entered it, muttering under his breath. Detective Rogers told Mister Finnegan to leave the body where it was and he'd make arrangements to have it collected first thing in the morning and have it delivered to the City Morgue. *"Just one more question..."* said Detective Mulligan, *"...what is the dead man's name"?* *"Jemmy O'Hare"* was the reply given. Mulligan wrote it down in his notebook and walked out of the pub with his police friends.

As soon as my mother heard Mister Finnegan coming up the stairs she ran into our other room, which we used as our kitchen, and put the kettle on for a cup of tea. Us three young ones were told to get into bed and go to sleep, only the adults were allowed into the kitchen. My two sisters slept at the foot of the big bed and my mother slept at the other end.

My bed was a type of fold down armchair that Mister Finnegan gave me. I remember the day himself and young Joe brought it up the stairs and the job they had in getting it into our room. *"Here you go...'* he said to me, *"...no more sleeping on that oul sack of straw for you"*. I was delighted of course because the straw bed was full of Fleas or Hoppers as my school pals used to call them. They'd have me eaten alive while I was asleep, sucking the blood out of my neck and leaving red blotches all over me.

My mother closed our bedroom door and the kitchen door as well and so all I heard was mumbling voices as I drifted off to sleep. Mister Finnegan and young Joe lived downstairs in the rooms at the back of the pub. My mother did all the cooking and cleaning for them and making up their beds, as well as doing all their washing.

The next morning was Sunday and I was getting ready to go out to ten o'clock Mass. My mother and the girls were still fast asleep as I quietly sneaked down the stairs into the pub. I gave a quick glance across at Jemmy to make sure he was still there. As I was reaching my hand out to pull the handle to open the pub door, the door suddenly sprung inwards and bashed me straight in the face, bursting my nose open and sending me sprawling backwards across the bar-room floor onto my back. In stormed the parents of Jemmy O'Hare.

There I was lying on the floor, gunner-eyed from the smack of the door and blood gushing down my clean, white

Sunday shirt. *"Where is he..."* screamed poor Misses O'Hare, *"...where's me son"*. Misses O'Hare had a stall in Moore Street where she sold apples and potatoes, her husband, Barney was a Dock Worker all his life and was never a man to be messed around with.

"Ah Jaysus Barney, look at our poor Jemmy" said Misses O'Hare, letting out a wail of a scream all over the pub. Standing behind her and looking over her shoulder, Mister O'Hare, in very solemn tones said, *"Someone's going to pay for this, mark my words, someone's going to pay for this"*. The screaming and wailing of poor Misses O'Hare had woken up my mother and Mister Finnegan, he came in from the backroom and my mother came down the stairs.

Mister Finnegan walked towards Mister O'Hare with his hand extended, they shook hands as Mister Finnegan broke the silence between these two old friends, *"Barney, I'm awful sorry about this, I was in behind the bar when it happened, there were three of them, that's all I can tell yeah"*. When Misses O'Hare saw my mother, she ran towards her and they threw their arms around each other, they were old pals from their school days, they held on to each other sobbing their hearts out.

Mister O'Hare was trembling with rage and anger. *"I'll have two of my boys come around later and bring him home for the burial, you and your son are welcome to come to the Wake of course"*, he said.

Mister Finnegan told him that the police had already been in and wanted Jemmy taken to the City Morgue. Misses O'Hare turned around and screamed out, *"He's coming home to us, this has nothing to do with them Rozzers"*. My mother had brought down a bedsheet from upstairs and with the help of Misses O'Hare, they covered over poor Jemmy. I was still lying on the floor while all this was going on. As Mister O'Hare stepped over me on his way out, he looked down and said, *"Sorry about that son"* and reaching down, placed a three-penny bit in my hand. My mother told me to go back upstairs and change my shirt.

While I was in the toilet, leaning over the little handbasin and washing the blood off my face, my sister Anne came running in and said *"Who boxed you in the face"?* She was then followed in by Mary, both of them still wearing their nightdresses that my mother had made for them.

I sat down on the edge of the toilet pot and told them what had happened. All the while, as they looked at me, they started giggling of course and I couldn't blame them, we didn't have a mirror or that so I couldn't see how bad my face looked. It was only when I was on my way to Mass that I caught my reflection in a shop window and saw how big my nose looked.

Everyone in the chapel kept looking around at me and whispering to each other. By this time, news of the shooting was all over our neighbourhood, everybody had heard some story or other about the shooting in the pub the night before. One little fella who was sitting with his mother in the seat in front of me kept glancing back at my big red nose. His mother would give a tug on the arm of his Jumper in an effort to make him sit quiet. *"But Ma'…"* he shouted all over the church *"…look at his nose"*. And with that of course, everyone else sitting nearby had to turn around and have a look and then they all began whispering about the shooting.

Father O'Sullivan turned around on the Altar and bellowed out, *"If I hear another word out of any of ye, I'll send ye all to Hell, now shut up"*. You could hear a Prayer Book drop with the silence. His Kerry accent always became more pronounced whenever he raised his voice. I couldn't help giggling to myself of course, at his use of the word ye because only Culchies used that word. In Dublin we always said youse, *"If I hear another word out of any of youse…"*

was the proper way to say it, not ye.

Outside after Mass some of my pals were asking me if I had been shot as well. I told them that when the bullet came out of the gun, it had skinned past my nose and that's what happened to me. Some of them wanted to touch it but I told them that it was still too sore. They were delighted with my story as they ran off down the street, they couldn't wait to tell all their pals about me being shot.

When I arrived back at the pub the place seemed quiet and eerie with Jemmy still lying under the white sheet on the bar counter. There was no one around, my mother had taken my sisters around to visit her own sister, my Auntie Rosie who lived in Gloucester Lane, she'd have some right stories to tell her now. Rosie was married to Ned-the-Liar and like Father O'Sullivan, he too was from the country. Whenever he'd go to tell people something or other, he'd always start off with, *"Now, I won't tell you a word of a lie"* and that was always taken as a sure sign that he was.

I went up to our room and was sitting on my armchair-bed reading a Comic when I heard shouting coming up from downstairs. I dropped my comic and ran out to the spy-hole on the Landing. I could see part of a policeman's uniform and the loudest voice I could hear was that of Mister O'Hare.

"You and your crew are not taking my son anywhere; he's coming home with us. Now, let that be the end of it. We'll sort this out without any help from Dublin Castle, thank you very much". The spy-hole was too restricting for me so I sneaked down the stairs and slightly opened the door into the bar.

As I squinted in through the opening, I could see Mister O'Hare and three of his sons and some of their cousins, standing inside the door. Further inside the pub were two men wearing white coats, like what a doctor or a butcher would wear, they were there to take the corpse away. In between the white coats and Mister O'Hare were four men in suits, detectives from Dublin Castle and behind them were several policemen.

One of the detectives spoke out with a strange accent which I later recognised as coming from Belfast. *"Now, Mister O'Hare...'* he said, *"...let's not make this situation any worse than it is. You know we have our work to do and we need to find the people who killed your son. So, please stand aside and let us get on with our job".* Mister O'Hare turned to his sons and they whispered amongst themselves. To me, it was almost like looking at the beginning of a gunfight from a Cowboy Film that I had seen on the Pictures.

It was then Mister O'Hare's turn to speak, *"Alright so..."* he said, *"...but I want him home in three days, no longer, is that understood"*. The detective nodded his head in a positive response, all the Cowboy's placed their guns back into their holsters and each one let out a great big sigh of relief as they prepared to mount their horses and ride off into the sunset.

Mister Finnegan came out of the backroom and stood behind the counter. The police headed out into the street, followed by the men in the white coats who had Jemmy on a stretcher. *"Well Barney..."* said Mister Finnegan, *"...what's it to be?"* The men standing at the pub door all turned in unison and looked at the barman. *"It's okay Barney, it's on the house, for the day that's in it, that is"*. All the men lined up against the bar as young Joe came out to give a hand.

Mister O'Hare spotted me and my big red nose peeping out from behind the door. He gave me a nod to come in and join the other lads. *"Here young Joe..."* he called across the counter, *"...give young Johnnie here a glass of red lemonade to match his nose..."* and then added, *"...on the house of course"*. This last comment split the tensed atmosphere and the lads all broke out laughing and began clapping each other on the back. I walked over and stood beside Mister O'Hare. He reached down and lifting me up, he put me sitting on the counter, next to where he was standing.

One of the lads standing next to Mister O'Hare suddenly spoke out, he was a First Cousin of Jemmy's. *"Well..."* he said, wiping the drippings of Stout from around his mouth onto his sleeve, *"...where do we go from here"?* A silence fell over the group of men. Each of them turned and looked along the bar at Mister O'Hare. He slowly turned his head and looking across the bar at Mister Finnegan, said *"Well old Joe, how do I answer that one"?*

There was a slight hesitation before an answer came, *"Let me make some inquiries, I'll talk to some friends of mine and we can take it from there. But let's bury young Jemmy first"* answered Mister Finnegan. All of the men nodded silently in agreement. I think myself that Mister Finnegan had anticipated that question coming up and was ready for it with his answer.

I was still sitting on the bar when I noticed Mister O'Hare giving a slight nod in the direction of Mister Finnegan. And then with their heads almost touching, Mister O'Hare whispered, *"My Jemmy wasn't an Informer, I brought him up, like the rest of my boys, knowing which side of his bread was buttered. He was no Informer I tell you".* Mister Finnegan repeated himself about making inquiries from his *"friends"* and the conversation ended there. Mister O'Hare stood upright and putting his cap on his head told the lads to finish up, they were going home.

"What did that word mean..."? I asked myself, *"...Informer"?* I had never heard that word before and why was Mister O'Hare whispering it into Mister Finnegan's ear, and what had it to do with Jemmy being shot"?

Although we had a door outside on the street that led into our downstairs hall, we seldom used it and instead we always came in and went out through the pub. And that's what my mother did just as all the lads were leaving. I could see my two sisters' trying to push their way in through the legs of the men.

Mister O'Hare tipped his cap when he saw my mother and walked on out of the pub. *"God love them all the same"* said my mother to no one in particular as she blessed herself. *"Amen to that"*, replied Mister Finnegan. I climbed down off the counter and followed my mother and sisters up the stairs. After clearing all the dirty glasses off the counter, the two Joe's went into the backroom.

I went back to reading my comic while my mother and my sisters went into the kitchen to make a start on the dinner. Every Sunday and at Mister Finnegan's insistence, we all had dinner together downstairs. He supplied us with most of the food and meat that we ate and he always had a bottle of wine on the dinner table every Sunday. He would give us little ones a small drop in a cup and himself, young Joe and my mother always had a full glass each.

Today was so much different than any other Sunday that I could remember. There was little or no conversation amongst the adults, which was most unusual. Mister Finnegan was asking the three of us little ones how we were doing in school. He told me that when I'm older he'd let me work in behind the bar with him and young Joe. He always promised the girls that when they grew up and were getting married, he would pay for their wedding. He would reassure my mother that as long as he was around, she'd always have a roof over her head. He was always such a kind and caring man to us.

True to their word and within three days, the police had released the body of Jemmy O'Hare for burial. His funeral was held in the Pro Cathedral. I remember the church was filled to capacity and they had to have the Service in the main chapel upstairs and not in the small side chapel downstairs where people were married. I went along to the church with my mother and sisters. Mister Finnegan had closed up the pub until the funeral was over. The one thing that I remember very clearly was the presence of about fifty uniform policemen all standing in and around the church.

For a moment I noticed Mister Finnegan talking with two men over by the side door and the next minute the men were gone, I remember wondering why they didn't stay for the whole funeral.

The funeral Mass itself seemed to go on for ever. Jemmy's brothers and his cousins all carried his coffin out through the church to the waiting hearse. When everything and everyone was ready, the driver cracked his whip and the four black horses, with their tall black feathery plumes moved off. The clattering metallic noise from their horseshoes echoed all along Marlborough Street as the funeral cortege headed out to Glasnevin Cemetery.

Some days later I arrived home from school as usual and was getting ready to go out on my rounds collecting empty Stout bottles. However, just as I was about to run down the stairs my mother called me. She was sitting in the kitchen having a cup of tea on her own. *"Mister Finnegan wants you to go with him on a very important message"* she said. *"Now, listen to me, you are to keep your mouth shut and you're to tell nobody anything about this, do you hear me. Go in and wash your face before you go down to him"?*

I just shrugged my shoulders, did what I was told and then headed off down the stairs to wait for Mister Finnegan. I wasn't too pushed about where I was going to go with him, he was probably just going to the doctor or something and didn't want anyone to know. I overheard him one time talking to my mother about his little problem. *"You've no idea of the pain I have to go through, it stings the life outta me when I'm in the toilet and especially if I have to get up outta my bed during the night".*

When Mister Finnegan came out of the backroom he was all cleaned up and shaved with a collar and tie on. He had just put his Overcoat on and then he ever so gently place his hat on his head so as not to disturb his hair. Now it was most unusual to see him dressed like this and especially when it wasn't a Sunday. During the week he always went about with his shirt sleeves rolled up to his elbows. That threw me a little alright. He just nodded at me and I headed out the door of the pub after him. He suddenly stopped walking and putting his hand on my shoulder said, *"Did your mother talk to you"?* I just nodded yes. And then we headed on down the street.

I walked along next to Mister Finnegan who was holding me by the hand. We turned right at the corner of the pub and went down Elliott Place and then we turned left into Purdon Street. Some of my pals from school were calling out to me to go and play with them. Some of them were going out to the North Strand for a ramble, I knew that meant they were going to rob apples out of someone's back garden.

Normally. I would have loved going off with them but Mister Finnegan had my hand in a firm grip. When we reached the end of Purdon Street, we walked across Beaver Street and out to Amiens Street and the train station.

We walked up the front steps of the station and out onto a platform. Mister Finnegan told me to sit on a seat while he went for some train tickets. Up to this point in my young life I had never before been on a train. The next thing I knew we were on the train and it was moving and we had a carriage all to ourselves. I was all excited at the idea of being on a moving train and being able to see out over all the rooftops of shops I was very familiar with and being able to look out over the railway bridge at the water of the River Liffey down below, where all the ships were tied up.

However, Mister Finnegan, who was sitting opposite me, had a very serious face on him and throughout our journey he never said one word to me until we eventually reached home many hours later that night.

The train seemed to go on for hours and hours but then it just came to a sudden halt. I must have dropped off to sleep at some stage of our journey. I stood up because Mister Finnegan stood up. He fixed himself and opening the carriage door, stepped out onto the platform, I followed. The platform was nothing like Amiens Street, it was all painted in lovely bright colours and had flowers growing everywhere. I then noticed a sign that said, *'Kingstown'*, I had no idea where we were.

Suddenly and almost as if he came out of nowhere, a man quickly approached us with his hand extended, Mister Finnegan took his hand and shook it. *"Billy, it's great to see you"* he said to the man. *"Likewise, Joe, likewise…,"* said his friend. *"…just the two of you then?"*, *"Yes and before you ask, I was very careful. That's why I brought the boy along, to throw the hounds off the track so to speak"*.

I had no idea what they were talking about or who, I certainly didn't see any hounds on our travels that day. We walked out of the train station and were directed to a waiting motor car. I couldn't believe it, imagine being on a moving train and in a real car all on the same day, wait till I tell my pals in school about this, I thought to myself.

But I never would because I suddenly remembered what my mother had said to me earlier that day, *"You are to keep your mouth shut and you're to tell nobody anything about this"*. So, why was I here I wondered to myself, why was I to keep my mouth shut about being on a moving train and in a motor car? Suddenly the car took off with a jerk and headed up through the town.

After a while I was starting to feel hungry and worse, I was bursting to do my Poolie. I was sitting in the back of the car on my own. Mister Finnegan and his friend were in the front, his friend was driving the car. I stood up and whispered in Mister Finnegan's ear. He asked his friend to stop somewhere for a few minutes. The three of us got out and I was directed to go behind a row of small bushes. I did my business as quickly as I could but it seemed to go on forever. When I came back to the car, I saw the two men standing over by some other bushes doing the same thing as I had just done. And so, it was back on the road and away we went.

We soon arrived at our destination, up along a very narrow Boreen, I could see a small cottage with a red tin roof and nobody around for miles, or so it seemed to me anyway. I noticed another car parked just at the side of the cottage. A dog started barking somewhere off in the distance as we were getting out of the car. We were brought inside the cottage door and at first it seemed very dark and gloomy.

I could just about make out three men sitting around a table and a woman standing over by the kitchen sink. A great big turf fire was blazing in the hearth. The three men stood up as we walked in and the woman immediately came over towards me. The men all shook hands with Mister Finnegan and sat round the table. The woman asked me my name and brought me over to a seat by the fire, where I sat with the driver. She served us all a cup of tea each and gave me a current bun to eat. I sat there staring into the flames, still not knowing why I was there or the purpose of our journey.

Having slept on the train I was quite alert and not tired. As I sat there looking into the fire, I had one ear cocked and listening to what was being said over at the table, I wanted to know why we were here. One of the men was speaking in a low voice and I was barely able to make out what was being said. *"Well Joe, our source of information from Dublin Castle was very definite about this. Let there be no mistake, we got the right man"*. A second man then spoke as he shoved some papers across the table to Mister Finnegan, *"Here's the evidence from the Castle, there's his name and code name and how much he was being paid, he was an Informer alright"*.

There was that word again, *'Informer'*, what did it mean? Mister Finnegan quickly stood up from the table and began pacing up and down in the small kitchen, he was muttering to himself. *"And you're sure there's no mistake, none at all"*? he asked. *"None at all, Joe, none at all"*, came the reply. *"Well…"* said Mister Finnegan, *"…that's it so, can I tell his father"*? *"Yes, you can but be discreet about it"*, said the first man.

Mister Finnegan reached across the table and taking up his hat placed it once more on his head. I stood up too because I knew that we were about to leave. The third man, who had said nothing since we came into the cottage, looked across the room at me and it was then, in the glow of the turf fire, that I recognised his face, even without his Gabardine Coat and Trilby Hat, I knew that he was the man who had almost tripped over me in the pub, he was the man who pulled the trigger and shot Jemmy. I stared at him for what seemed forever. He grinned and gave me a wink of acknowledgement, as if both him and I had played a role in the murder of Jemmy O'Hare.

Mister Finnegan said his thanks and goodbyes and we headed back to Kingstown and the train home. It was dark when we arrived back in Amiens Street. There was nothing said by either one of us on our homeward journey. I just knew that I had to find out what the word *'Informer'* meant but who could I ask that wouldn't give the game away on me? When we reached Railway Street and came to the door of the pub Mister Finnegan stopped and looking down at me said *"Remember what your mother told you earlier. Now, be a good boy"*. He then handed me a sixpenny bit. I put it in my pocket straightaway. My silence was paid for. We then walked into a very noisy pub and I went straight upstairs.

My mother was sitting up in bed reading a book, my two sisters were fast asleep. When I walked into the room my mother looked up at me and said *"You must be tired, you had a long day. Would you like some Hot Cocoa"?* I didn't have the energy to say anything and so I just nodded. I folded my bed down and fixed the sheet and blanket on it before crawling into it, I felt exhausted. My mother soon brough back a mug of Hot Cocoa. I sat up and silently drank it.

Soon enough my mother returned to her bed. Having turned the light out, she lay down to sleep. I listened to her breathing as it became shallower by the minute and then evened out as she fell into a deep sleep. As I lay in my bed that night I just couldn't sleep, I wanted to know what that word meant and how it was connected to Jemmy O'Hare. Why was he shot dead because of the word *'Informer'?*

A few days later, as I was walking home from school with some of my pals, I saw Mister Finnegan standing on the corner of Rutland Street and Gloucester Street. Now, this was very strange indeed, what was he doing there, I wondered. There must be something wrong with my mother, I thought.

I looked over at Mister Finnegan and he nodded for me to cross over the road to him. As I stood there looking up at him, I said *"Is me Ma' alright Mister Finnegan?"*. He took me by the hand and walked a few paces before stopping. *"Yes, she's grand. I need you to do something for me. I want you to call in to Mister O'Hare and tell him to come to the pub, tell him I have some news for him. Now..."*, he whispered, *"...remember what your mother told you about our little trip away, say nothing of this to no one"*. I nodded in response.

I knew from collecting the Stout Bottles that Mister O'Hare lived in number 7 Faithful Place, just off Railway

117

Street and that he lived in the same house as Mister and Misses McDermot, one family lived upstairs and the other family lived downstairs in the one house. Mister McDermot worked in the Corporation, he used to go around with a long pole and he was able to light the street lamps with it, I heard some of the men in the pub calling him a *"Glimmer Man"* but I never knew what that meant.

I knew he wasn't a Protestant or that because I used to see him and Misses McDermot at Mass every Sunday and he used to hand around the collection box for the priest. And so, I gave Mister Finnegan my schoolbag to bring home for me and off I ran towards Faithful Place.

The O'Hare's lived in the downstairs front parlour of number ten and so I knocked on the window, the same as I used to do when I was collecting the empty Stout Bottles. Misses O'Hare pulled back one side of the net curtain and looked out at me with a puzzled look on her face. *"We have no empty bottles today love"* she shouted out at me.

I leaned over close to the window so nobody would hear what I had to say. *"I have a message for Mister O'Hare"* I whispered. *"You want a what"?* she shouted back. In exasperation I roared back at her, *"Open the door"*. Well, the next thing is, Misses McDermot is hanging out of the top window looking down at me. *"Here son..."* she says, *"...she's a bit on the deaf side, you'll have to shout a bit louder"*.

Suddenly Misses O'Hare opens up her window and peering out said *"We have no empty bottle today love"*. Her breath was reeking of boiled cabbage and Pig's Feet. The smell coming out through her Front Parlour window was the same kind of smell that I remembered from the tenement house we used to live in.

It was then that Mister O'Hare came to the window with a knife and fork in one hand and moved his wife to one side. I looked at him and said *"Mister Finnegan has a message for you and he's in the pub"*. Without another word being exchanged between us, the window was closed and Mister O'Hare was out on the street in a flash and still chomping on a mouth full of dinner.

At the speed Mister O'Hare was walking it took only a few minutes for us to reach the door of the pub. Mister Finnegan looked busy cleaning and wiping down tables and the counter of the bar. He looked over his shoulder to see who had come into the pub. Mister O'Hare said *"I'm here Joe"*. Mister Finnegan directed him towards the backroom and looking over at me, told me to put the bottom bolt on the door and to close the latch tight so that no one could come into the pub and disturb them. I did as I was told and now that my part in the plot was over, I rambled on upstairs to do my Ecker or School Homework as it is now called.

In a way I was fuming at Mister Finnegan for going into the backroom because I was planning on listening down through the spy hole at what was being said. My mother was sitting on the edge of her bed sewing and fixing some thing or other belonging to one of my sisters. The girls were sitting on the floor over by the window playing with their dolls. I picked up my schoolbag and walked across the hallway into the kitchen. When I finished my sums, I put my head down on the table and fell asleep.

The noise of a door closing woke me up. I could see across to our bedroom and my mother and the girls were still there. I crept out quietly to the hallway and peeped down through the spy hole. I couldn't see anyone but I did recognise the voices of Mister Finnegan and Mister O'Hare. *"Will you have a whiskey before you go"* said Mister Finnegan. *"Ah sure I might as well, for the day that's in it anyhow"*, answered Mister O'Hare. Everything went quiet, just the sound of liquid pouring into glasses. Then Mister O'Hare spoke, *"Well, that's that so, how am I going to explain this to the Misses and the boys. I don't know what I'm going to say, we'll have to move to England"*.

Mister Finnegan handed him a glass of whiskey and said *"It may not have to come to that, I have a brother down in Wexford who might help out with a place for you and the family. The lads could help him on the farm or something"*. Mister O'Hare gulped down some of the whiskey and answered, *"You're a good man Joe, but I think England is the only option left to us. I have a cousin named Matt who lives over there in Birmingham, he'll help us out"*.

Mister Finnegan then asked a question, *"Were you and the Misses never suspicious as to where his money was coming from"*? Mister O'Hare quietly put his empty glass down on the counter. *"Yes, we did wonder of course but he always had an answer, no matter what the question was. Sure, herself couldn't sleep at times worrying about it. I had warned my boys against taking stuff from off the Docks in case they'd lose their jobs over it, we just didn't know, and that's being honest"*. And that's how they left it. The two men shook hands and Mister O'Hare walked out of the pub all slouched up, as if he had the weight of the world and its mother resting on his shoulders, we never saw him or his family again.

The following Saturday I made my way over to the Church; I was going to Confession. It's not that I had much to tell the priest or that, I just had a question I wanted to ask him. The church was almost empty when I walked in after blessing myself with some Holy Water.

Misses Boyle was kneeling in her usual position up near the Altar, saying her Rosary. Misses Mac was busying herself polishing the great big brass candle holders nearby. Ever since her husband died, she had volunteered to clean the church every Saturday in preparation for Sunday Mass.

Poor oul Mister Nolan was sitting over by the statue of the Blessed Virgin because he had nowhere else to go, he told my mother one time that he didn't like staying in his tenement room on his own so much. He told her that sometimes Holy Mary would talk to him.

There were two young girls waiting to go into the Confession Box ahead of me. I think one of them suffered with her nerves because she kept fixing her scarf and asking her pal was it straight. The priest, Father O'Sullivan, shoved his head out of the Confession Box and told her to be quiet. Soon enough my turn came. I had no idea as to how I was going to start so I just opened my mouth as soon as the priest pulled across the wooden window. *"Father..."* I blurted out,

"...I don't have any sins to tell you, I just wany to know is it a sin to call someone an Informer"? Now there, it was out.

I could see the bulging eyes and the red face of the priest pressed up against the metal grill that divided us. *"WHAT!!!"* he roared in at me in his Kerry accent. With the fright and the spit that came out of his mouth, I lost my balance and fell back. *"Where did you hear that from..."* he demanded. *"...don't you know that's worse than committing ten Mortal Sins"*?

The next thing was the door of the Confession Box was pulled open and there stood the Priest, towering over me. At first, I thought there were two Priests because he had moved so quickly out from his seat. He reached in and catching me by the scruff of the neck, he pulled me out of the Confession Box.

I was frog-marched into the Sacristy and told to sit down. Father O'Sullivan pulled up a chair and sat facing me. *"Now..."* he said in a low voice, *"... you had better tell me who you heard being called an Informer"*. I wasn't sure what to say. *"Hurry up..."* he said, *"...or I'll make sure you roast in Hell"*. I sat there shaking in my seat and feeling a nice warm watery sensation dribbling down my leg, what do I say and how do I get out of this in one piece? *"Are you still* hearing my Confession Father..." I asked him, "...because if you are, I can tell you and you can't tell anyone else". The next thing was, he stood up and changing out of his robes, he put on his coat and scarf.

The priest had a good tight grip on my arm as we headed off over to the pub. "I want to talk to your mother about this, so I do young man" he said, almost out of breath. That was when I knew I was in deep trouble because as sure as anything my mother would tell Mister Finnegan about it and he'd want to know anyway because he'd most probably see the priest hauling me in through the pub and up the stairs.

And what would any of my pals think if they saw the priest hauling me around by the arm? When we arrived in the pub there were a few of the regular customers seated about the place. They all looked up when the priest barged in with me in tow. As the priest reached out to open the door leading to our stairs Mister Finnegan called out. "Eh Father O'Sullivan, I think you might be better off bringing him out to the back". The priest looked across the room at Mister Finnegan who was pointing a finger at the door behind the bar. "Right so" said the priest and in we went behind the bar and through the open door.

Mister Finnegan walked in behind us with a bottle of whiskey in one hand and two glasses in the other. He told me to sit over on the settee by the fireplace and beckoned to Father O'Sullivan to take a seat at the table in the middle of the floor.

He then sat down himself and proceeded to fill up the two glasses from the bottle in complete silence. After sipping a drop of the whiskey Father O'Sullivan went to say something but Mister Finnegan raised his hand in protest and the priest stopped in mid-sentence.

Mister Finnegan then looked across the room in my direction and said, *"You see Father, it's like this. Now, if I for instance told you something in Confession and you went and told it to your Bishop, you would become known as an Informer because you weren't supposed to tell anyone what I had told you. You informed your Bishop and you shouldn't have. Is that right"*? The priest looked across at me before giving an answer. *"Yes, technically I suppose you're right Mister Finnegan"*, he said. *"And..."*, continued Mister Finnegan, *"...if I told young Johnnie here something and let him know that he wasn't to spout a word of it to anyone else and if he did, then he too could be called an Informer, is that right"*? *"That's also right..."* said the priest, *"... and for*

125

doing such a thing or calling somebody such a name, he could end up in Hell for a very long time because that's worse than committing at least ten Mortal Sins.".

I could feel beads of sweat dripping down my face, I was terrified in case the priest sent me down to Hell and what would my mother think? She' be worried as to what the neighbours might say. *"Well..."* said Mister Finnegan, *"...I think we can leave it there for now".* *"Certainly"* said the priest. Father O'Sullivan stood up to leave the room and as he did so, he reached his hand out across the table and took up the bottle of whiskey. *"I'll be sure to keep this safe for you Mister Finnegan"* he said and off he went with the bottle hidden under his coat.

Mister Finnegan stood up, closed the door behind the priest and walking over to the sofa, sat down beside me. I started crying and through my tears I told Mister Finnegan I was very sorry for what I had done and that I'd never do it again. I told him I hated being an Informer.

Mister Finnegan looked down at me and asked, *"What's an Informer then"?* I looked up at him and said, *"It's just another word for someone who squeals on their pals"* He put his arm around me and pulled me in close to his side. *"Now you have it, just remember it's also a bad word and*

Father McDermot said it's worse than ten Mortal Sins". As he looked down at my tear-streaked face he said, *"Are we still best pals then."*? I told him that we'd always be best pals and snuggled in to him a little bit more.

Dying Embers

When I was ten years old my Da' was a giant of a man. Sometimes when he came home from the pub, he would show me how he could nearly reach up to the sky by standing on his tippy toes. And there were times I remember when he would lift me up onto his shoulders and I could see for miles around our tenement room. There was one corner up near the ceiling where a great big spider had a cobweb and my Da' would give me his oul cap and tell me to knock it flying and I would. I loved me oul Da' and especially when he'd come in from the pub full of drink and he'd give me and my little brother and my little sister a handful of change out of his pocket and send us off to the shops to buy ourselves bags of sweets.

Sometimes when I'd be in bed late at night, I would hear him singing at the top of his voice as he stumbled and tripped and made his way up the darkened stairs in the tenement house, we lived in. Our house was just around the corner from Faithful Place. He used to be able to get some work down on the docks with his pals offloading a ship's cargo or shovelling tons of coal out of an oul boat. He always looked funny when he came home from working on the coal boat because his face was always black from the coal dust.

I used to see him putting a few pound notes into his shoe before he'd hand my Ma' the rest of his money, she didn't see him doing it of course but I was always sure that she knew. I know now that times were very hard for them and especially when there was no work for me Da'. Of an evening, him and my Ma' would sit by the fire and try to work out between them, what they could do. When I'd be saying my prayers before I got into bed every night, I'd ask Holy Mary and Baby Jesus to please help the Ma' and Da' but I don't think that they ever listened to me, probably because I was such a small little skinny boy and not worth bothering with, but I asked them anyway.

Myself and my brother and sister slept together on a flour bag filled with oul straw and we had my Da's overcoat over us to keep us warm. My Ma' and Da' slept in a single bed with two blankets. We had one chair with no back on it and a small stool to sit on. We also had two Tea Chests that the Da' brought home from the Docks one day. One of them was for keeping our clothes in and the other was for the few pieces of delph and plates that we had.

My Ma' was much smaller than my Da' and she was very skinny. She always seemed to cough a lot and especially when she would get a cigarette from Mrs Doran who lived across the landing from our room. She was always very good to the Ma', sometimes she would bring in a loaf of bread or a few pig's feet for us to eat and she'd never ask the Ma' for money or anything like that. Her husband worked in Dublin Corporation. They gave him a bicycle to go around on because he used to have to listen out for water that was dripping in any of the shores and that.

I remember seeing him one time and he bent over with his ear pressed up against the long piece of pipe that he had shoved down a shore outside our house and when I asked him what he was doing, he told me he was listening out for any burst water pipes. I had no idea what he was talking about, sure how could he tell if a pipe was burst if he couldn't see the water spilling out onto the road? Anyway, the Ma' told me one time that Mister Doran was a decent man because he didn't drink or smoke like my Da' did and that's why they always had money to spare.

I remember one time when my Da' took me and my brother out for a walk one day down by the Liffey, he wanted to show us all the boats that were docked along the quays. We stopped at the steps of the Custom House to watch some of his pals playing a game called *"The Toss"*, I didn't understand it at the time because all they were doing was throwing money up in the air and shouting at each other when it landed on the ground. My Da' called it a mug's game. My brother was one year younger than me and his name was Padso and my sister was a year younger than him and she was called Maureen.

There was one night in particular that I will never forget. We were all in bed and the wind was howling outside our window like an oul Banshee and the rain was lashing down with the force of a hurricane. All through the night my poor Ma' was coughin' and barkin' non-stop. My Da' kept getting up out of bed and giving her mugs of water to drink. The water came from a tap down in the backyard and was kept in a bucket over by our window. I couldn't sleep with all the coughing and all.

My Ma' eventually got up out of bed and sat on the stool over beside the fireplace. I got up as well and started blowing at the dying embers to try and bring them back to life so that the Ma' could get a heat, I even tore up a comic that I had and put it in the fire. I didn't understand in those early years of my young life why my mother was coughing up blood and spitting it into the fire, I knew nothing of anything like that.

And so, the next morning my Da' sent me across the landing to get Misses Doran and tell her that my Ma' needed her help. And without hesitation Misses Doran dropped everything that she was doing, told her husband he'd have to get his own breakfast and grabbing her headscarf, pushed me out the door and back across the landing into our room. My poor Ma' looked like a bag of old bones lying on the bed with her dark eyes set back into her shrunken face. She didn't even have the energy to speak to Misses Doran. My poor oul Da' didn't know what to be doing and I knew by looking at him that he wanted to cry but he wouldn't in case us little ones got upset. Misses Doran looked across the semi darkened room at him and said *"Paddy, you better get a priest, I don't think she has much time left"*.

I remember standing over by the window and seeing my father moving, almost in slow motion, as he raised himself up of the floor. His eyes were all glazed over as he glanced in my direction and said *"You stay here and look after Padso and Maureen, that's a good boy"*. I couldn't speak, not a word came out of my mouth, I was suddenly frozen solid and unable to move an inch. I didn't understand what was happening and why I was feeling the way that I was but I somehow sensed a great big dark cloud descending on the scene before my childish eyes.

The rain and the wind had blocked out all sense of light to our room. Misses Doran went away for a few minutes and eventually came back with a bottle of Holy Water from Lourdes, a lighted candle and a Holy Cross with Jesus on it. She placed them on the stool next to my mother's bed. Padso and Maureen were crying non-stop into the oul straw bed. I was still unable to move, I was lost in a twilights zone. Misses Doran was standing over my Ma', making a sign of the Cross with the Holy Water and reciting one prayer after another, while she held my Ma's hand.

It was soon enough when I heard my father's voice from the hallway downstairs. He had someone with him, it was the Priest. On the landing outside our door, I could see some of our other neighbours, all with sad and worried faces on them and continually blessing themselves while they prayed. I remember hearing Mister Walsh reciting the Rosary, he was easy to pick out because he was a tall man who towered over everyone else, he used to go to Mass every morning on his way into work.

The Priest and my Da' made their way through to our room. The Priest started saying prayers in Latin, well at least I thought it was Latin because that's how the Mass was said every Sunday.

My poor mother never said a word, she had no strength left in her body. My Da' knelt beside the bed and taking her hand in his said to her *"Chrissie, you were my first and only love. Do you remember the May Procession we were in together and we kept looking over at each other? I got my first job on a Messenger Bike when I was fourteen and I asked you out to the Pictures and your man wouldn't let us in because you were only twelve. We stuck together through thick and thin even though your father didn't approve of us getting married. Chrissie, what am I going to do without yeah"?*

And then he broke down and cried and so did all our neighbours and the Priest as well. My poor Ma' never opened her eyes again, she was gone up to Heaven. I lay down on the sacking next to Padso and Maureen and put my arms around them, we sobbed our little hearts out.

I have no recollection of my mother's funeral; I remember I did kiss her as she lay in her coffin and when nobody was looking, I took a scissors out of my pocket and snipped a little piece of her hair off and put it in my pocket next to the scissors. that's all the memory I have left of that dreadful day in my young life. I still have that little piece of my mother's hair but I keep it in a small envelope now. I take it out every now and then while sitting on my own and I have a little chat with her about this, that and the other.

I remember what my Da' was like after she died. Whenever he'd come home with a few drinks on him he would shout up the stairs, *"I'm home Chrissie, is the kettle on"*? All that ever came back to him was an eerie silence. He'd make his way up the stairs singing to himself, *"Your eyes were blue, your haired was curled, when first we fell in love"*, she loved him singing that song and sometimes she'd even join in on the chorus. Then he would throw his arms

135

around her and they'd give each other a great big kiss on the lips. That's when we'd start shouting, *"Ah here, stop that carrying on"* and we'd all break out into roars of laughter. Within two years of my mother's death my poor oul Da' sadly passed away, he died of a broken heart, that's what the nurse in the hospital told us.

My Auntie May, she was my father's sister, took Padso and Maureen in to live with her and her three young children. They lived in a house up on the Cabra Road and they even had a back garden. May was married to Ernie Gallagher, he was an Irish speaker from County Donegal and he worked in the Civil Service. He had to wear a suit to work every day. I moved in with my Granny Burke, she lived in a small cottage down a laneway off Beaver Street. It wasn't until I moved in with her that I discovered she smoked a pipe.

My granny was a small little woman with a slight country accent. She said she was born in the mountains of Slievenamon in County Tipperary. She told me that her father used to make the Poitín for all his neighbours and that her own mother could tell people their fortune by reading their Tea Leaves. There was a Fairy Fort at the back of their cottage that was supposed to be haunted or so she told me.

I left school at fourteen years of age, barely able to read or write. I found it hard to get a job at first. One of my pals would sometimes let me help him sell newspapers around all the pubs near where we lived. I remember a good few of the boys who sold papers for a living had no shoes to wear. In the winter a boy would put his cap on the ground and stand on it to try and keep his feet warm. In time, one of the newspapers started up a fund for money to buy shoes for the young paper sellers.

I remember one time when this other boy asked me to help him sell his papers. All along the docks there were many ships and boats tied up and we went along the Quay selling his newspapers to the men who worked on these boats. There was one boat in particular that I remember we stopped at and he called out *"Herald or Mail, get your newspaper"*.

There was no sign of anyone onboard. He looked at the boat and then looked at me and said, *"Here... ",* and gave me his pile of papers to hold, *"...I won't be a minute"* and off he went up the gangplank and boarded the boat. I could hear him calling out, *"Hello, anyone here"* and then a door would slam. Soon enough he was back by my side. *"Here... "*, he told me, *"...put them in your pocket for later".* He handed me several packets of cigarettes and boxes of matches. He told me that he found some money as well and would share it with me later but I was to keep my mouth shut.

These are just some of the things I think about when I'm out strolling around Dublin on my own. It might seem strange but every corner I turn around there's a story waiting to meet me. It's almost like bumping into an old pal that I haven't seen for years. Sometimes it might be a building or a shop that calls me and says *"Howya, do you remember the story about me"*? And off I'd go talking to my other self and smiling at some of what I'd remember. There are often times when I'd be letten on I was walking with me Ma' and Da' and they telling me all their stories over and over again.

Now, don't be telling anyone this but I'd sometimes have a little cry to myself because I miss them so much. I often wonder when I'd see other people like me strolling along, were they doing the same thing as me, talking to themselves about when they were young. What I do know is that I had the best Ma' and Da' ever, they loved us kids and they loved each other.

The Last Trip Home

My name is Johnnie Carroll and I had decided to visit Dublin, the place of my birth, for one last time, after an absence of more than twenty years. I could easily have flown home I suppose, but in my head, I had convinced myself that if I left on the boat then I should return on the boat. I was twenty-three years old when my father had passed away, two months before my mother. The doctor said it was the fags, the cigarettes, that took my father, his lungs were riddled with cancer.

Thankfully in some way, he went quickly, that's the way he would have wanted it. He was never one for beating about the bush and in the middle of some argument with one of his pals or other he'd shout out *"For God's sake, will you ever get to the point and stop beating about the bush"*. That was him, I'm probably a little bit like that myself, if I'm being honest.

When I was growing up, we lived in the top back room in our house, a great big old tenement house on the corner of Railway Street and White's Lane, directly across from the original school in Railway Street. Ours was the cheapest room in the house, the only one my mother and father could afford, seeing as how he wasn't always working. I well remember as a little boy having to climb each and every step all the way up to the top landing and my poor leg muscles would be aching and paining me for hours afterwards.

An older boy in my school told me that our house used to be haunted by a woman dressed all in white and that she would stand at the top of the first flight of stairs howling and crying with a baby in her arms. The neighbours had to get the priest to bless the stairs and that got rid of her. Our house had a permanent smell, I can remember it very clearly but how to describe it is another thing altogether. I could say it smelled of boiled cabbage, fried eggs, human sweat and piss, excuse the language, but that would only be putting it very mildly, it was worse than that.

In school you could always tell which tenement house someone lived in by the smell off their clothes and we were no different. I remember one time two Young Ones were looking at me and saying *"He smells like he lives in number thirty-five"* and they were right.

My father would get a few days' work here and there, sometimes down on the docks offloading a ship full of wheat that would come in on the high tide from Canada. Other times he might get a week's work going off down to the country as a helper on a lorry collecting dead horses. I remember when he sailed over to Chester in England with one of his pals to collect a consignment of red bricks that were being used to build some of the new Corporation houses and shops that were springing up around the suburbs of Dublin.

He came home this time and told my mother that he was going over to England to bring a load of bricks back. *"Me oul pal, Paddy Coffey has offered me a bit of work on his boat, we're going over to Chester and I'll be gone for three or four days"*. My mother looked at him and said *"Sure you can't sail in a boat, you'd get sea sick crossing the bridge out in Dollymount".*

But my father was more determined than ever and true enough, off he sailed. My mother and her pal, Chrissie Nolan brought me and my younger twin brothers, Tommy and Jimmy and our little sister Vera, across to City Quay to watch my father sailing off into the sunset, the boat had barely moved and he was already hanging over the side. The twins were crying because they thought my father was never going to come back. One thing I can honestly say about him, is that he was never afraid of work, when he could get it that is and especially if it was handy.

I remember my Auntie Polly, that's my father's younger sister, she was married to Fingers O'Shea. I never knew his real name back then because everyone always called him Fingers. Seemingly, when he was fifteen, he lost three fingers off his right hand during the war with the Black and Tans.

According to my father he was lobbing a hand grenade into the back of a *"Tan"* lorry as it was going down Talbot Street and the grenade blew up just as he threw it and it took off three of his fingers. In all the confusion of the blast an Oul One wrapped her black shawl around his head and shoulders and along with her pal, they brought him to the Dispensary up on Summerhill to a doctor. They couldn't chance bringing him to Jervis Street Hospital as they knew there were always Policemen and Soldiers hanging around outside and they might be caught but he had lost the three fingers and that's how he got that name. He didn't have to work, because he got a pension from the new Irish Government for fighting the Black and Tans.

Polly would sometimes take me along with her if she was going for a message or that. She used to take me with her if she was bringing a Billy Can full of tea down to my father who would sometimes be waiting at the Customs House to see if there was any chance of a bit of work going in any of the old Coal Yards across the river along City Quay. Polly was very fond of my father, there was only the two of them left. Their own father died when they were very young and they had a sister as well who was born in between the two of them.

When their mother died four years after their father, the Parish Priest handed them in to the Magdalene Sisters in Sean McDermot Street. After a number of months their Granny went to the Parish Priest and told him that she would do the rearing of the children. So, off they went to collect the three little ones but the head Nun said that they had only handed in two children, they never saw their sister again.

Polly and Fingers had no children of their own. They lived in a room in number 11 Elliott Place, that was Misses Doyle's house, they had the front parlour downstairs. The room was only big enough for a single bed and a small table and it had a little fireplace as well. There was a picture of the Sacred Heart up on the wall over the bed.

Polly and Fingers used to always say the Rosary every night before they got into bed and they'd make me kneel down beside them and say it as well. I remember that they used to let me sleep in between the two of them. Polly would let me cuddle into her and she'd be kissing me on my forehead, I clearly remember feeling so loved and safe back then.

My father told me that Polly had given birth to a little girl shortly after she was married. The baby was born in our room, my mother delivered it. My father said that the baby was born weak and only lived for about four or five days. My mother had sent for the priest to come around and baptise the little infant, the baby was too weak to be brought to the church.

My father seemed to remember everything about that time as though it had happened only yesterday. Himself and Fingers brought the little one up to Glasnevin to be buried. They walked up from Railway Street with a little bundle wrapped up in half a bedsheet, Fingers carried it all the way to the cemetery gates and had cried non-stop at the loss of his little child.

I didn't really understand it when my father told me that Polly wasn't allowed to go with them to the graveyard. He said that's just the way it was back then. My mother would have stood at the door of our tenement house with her arms tightly wrapped around poor Polly as she sobbed her heart out at the loss of her little girl. I suppose my mother had a cry as well but she probably would have done it while Polly wasn't around because she wouldn't want to upset her any more than she already was.

My father and Fingers went into *"The Gravediggers"* pub afterwards and my father ended up practically having to carry Fingers home because he was so upset and full of drink. The baby was never mentioned again but they did give her a name, she was called Theresa, because she was born on the Feast Day of Saint Theresa. She was buried in the Angel's Plot along with all the other little babies.

In the darkness of their little room, Fingers would sit up in the bed with a cigarette in his mouth and every time he'd take a drag on it the whole room would light up all red. It reminded me of the lighthouse out in Ringsend that we could see all the way over from Dollymount. My father used to bring me out to Dollyer on the crossbar of his bike at night to show me the light beaming across the water from the lighthouse.

Fingers would puff out a great big cloud of cigarette smoke up towards the ceiling and then, drawing in a deep breath, he would begin to tell myself and Polly stories about his time in the IRA and how his own father had been sent to prison for helping to bring guns into Dublin from a boat out in Howth. Fingers had a never-ending supply of great stories about when he was a young fella. I'd soon fall asleep with rifles and Black and Tans and soldiers running around inside my little head, chasing after Fingers and his father.

Polly loved that little room, she kept it so clean and tidy and because it was so small everything had its place. Sometimes she'd send me out to the backyard with the po that she kept under the bed; my father used to call it *"A Gusunder"* because it goes under the bed. I'd throw the Poolie down the shore and clean out the po under the water tap. When Polly wasn't in work, she would spend hours looking out her front window at all the business of the street and sometimes one or two of her oul pals might sit on the window sill outside, it was really low down you see and she'd have her window open and they be chatting for hours on end.

Polly worked three days a week for Mitchell's Rosary Bead factory over in Waterford Street, it was in behind the Dandy garage. She mainly worked in the grinding room where she would have to grind all the Crosses down to a certain size for to fit on the Rosary Beads. The other women didn't like it if they were told to work in the grinding room because of the dust getting into their hair and down their throats. Polly didn't mind because she was paid extra for working in there.

I remember Mister Enright, he lived in the room up above Polly's room, he was a Protestant from Belfast. Sometimes when he was drunk, he'd open his window and play his mouth organ, the sound of it would be heard all over the street. He'd lean right out and play *"The Sash me Father Wore"*, just to annoy all his neighbours. Nobody ever paid any heed to him and his oul *"Orange tunes"*. If you saw him coming back from Misses Kane's shop, he'd be like a little mouse walking in close to the wall. Sometimes, if there was a bit of a hooley in the street he'd lean out his window and play a few Irish tunes for all the Oul Ones to dance to.

Unknown to me at that time of my young life, some of the houses in Railway Street were what was then known as Brothels. The women that lived in these houses walked the streets at night in search of men who would pay them for their services. In fact, as I was to discover in much later years, almost every house in the area where I grew up had a Brothel or a Shebeen or maybe both.

When I was about twelve years of age I began working for Misses Doyle, she ran some of these types of houses in Elliott Place and some of the ones around the far corner in Purdon Street, she owned quite a number of houses in the area. She told me that I had to make sure to go to school every day and if I would she'd give me a few jobs to do for her and pay me for doing them.

My main job was to sweep down the stairs and hallways of four houses in Elliott Place, number three, number six, number ten and number fourteen where she lived. I also had to make sure that the backyard of each house was clean and tidy. She got a man in one time to knock down the wall at the back of the yard in number fourteen and I had to help

148

him. The wall was taken down so that in the event of a police raid on her Shebeen,

Misses Doyle's customers would run out to the backyard and cut in through the back door of the house at the back where the wall used to be, they would all come out at the front through number 5 Byrne's Square, she owned that house as well. By the time the hall door in Elliott Place was knocked in by the police, all of Misses Doyle's customers would be long gone.

By going in and out of these houses I got to know most of the women. Now, my father would never call them that, he always referred to them as *"The Girls"*. I worked up a nice little business with the help of some of the girls. Anytime that they had a man in they'd give me a shout and ask me to go to the pub and bring back a few bottles of stout, your man paid them, of course but any change left over from buying the beer always ended up in my pocket, your man never got it. According to the Brothel Madam, once a girl had a customer in her room, she was never allowed to leave the house on her own and that's how I was always asked to run and fetch for them.

Most of these houses had one or maybe two *"Strong Men"* who stood out at the hall door, especially at night time when business was in full flow. They each carried a set of knuckle dusters, a cut-throat razor and a length of lead pipe. Sometimes one or two of them might even carry a gun. They were there to carry out the Madam's orders, be it beating up a customer who was maybe a little slow in paying up for services rendered or dealing with a girl who got out of line.

Sometimes the girls were beaten up and then slashed on their arm with a razor as a warning, not only to her but to any other girl who might be a bit troublesome. If a girl continued stepping out of line, she was likely to be slashed across the face with a razor. Once a girl lost her good looks or was marked in this way, she was thrown out onto the street and would find it very hard to make ends meet.

My own mother was a quiet enough woman, she had no family. She knew nothing of her birth parents or if she had any brothers or sisters. You see, when she was a baby, she was abandoned by her own mother who left her behind the hall door of a tenement house in Railway Street, she was no more than three weeks old. She told me that Mister and Misses Hayes found her lying there crying from the hunger.

Now, this couple already had ten children of their own, seven boys and three girls and straightaway they decided to keep my mother and rear her as their own. Much later on

Misses Hayes told my mother what happened. *"We had just slipped out for a quick drink in Phil Shanahan's pub that night. All my husband's shipmates were in there and I was in the Snug with some of my own pals. I remember it was raining when we were coming home and I had my scarf on. As we stepped into the hall of our house, I could hear a crying sound. I gripped Tom by the arm and asked him if it was a Banshee or what".*

Misses Hayes told my mother that they both stood still when they got to the first step on the stairs leading up to their room. Tom was afraid of nothing she said and was ready for action if anyone tried to attack them. It was then that he looked over his shoulder and saw a little bundle lying on the floor behind the doorway of their tenement house. *"A Jaysus Maureen..."* he said, *"...what's that on the floor"?* Misses Hayes told my mother that when she bent down, she saw a little child all wrapped up in a black shawl and that it was like looking at the Baby Jesus in his crib on Christmas morning. Mister Hayes then said to his wife, *"Take that child upstairs Maureen and we'll work something out in the morning".*

And that's how it happened, my mother was baptised a couple of days later in the Pro Cathedral and given the name

Mary Hayes. She told me that she couldn't have wished for better parents or a better family because they all played a role in her upbringing. She said that her brothers would never let anyone pick a fight with her or push her around and her sisters were the same.

My mother remembered the day when she made her First Holy Communion and how Misses Hayes was crying her eyes out with happiness when she saw her walking back from the Altar with her hands joined in prayer and looking like a little Angel. Mister Hayes and his two eldest sons were always away at sea. His youngest son worked on the cattle boat, the emigrants ship to England.

A few days after my fourteenth birthday I woke up to see my mother standing beside my bed and looking down at me. At first, I wasn't too sure if I was actually awake or still asleep. *"Get up and wash your face..."* she said, *"...I'm taking you to see the Priest"*. I quickly sat up in the bed because I wasn't too sure as to what I had just heard and asked her, *"What Priest?"*. She glared at me and said, *"Never mind what Priest, just get up and do what you're told"*.

My poor head was spinning in an attempt to try and remember what sins I had committed and forgotten to tell in

152

Confession. My two younger brothers were still fast asleep at the end of the bed and my father was gone off somewhere or other, my little sister was asleep over in the corner of our room, on the floor, lying on the sack of straw that she called her bed.

I quickly gulped down a cup of scalding hot tea at the same time as I was combing my hair. My mother was impatiently standing by the door of our room with her coat and scarf on. I still had no idea what was going on. It was eleven o'clock on a miserable Saturday morning in February. It was raining of course, a misty sort of rain, the kind that soaks you through to the skin before you know where you are.

I remember we walked in silence across Gardiner Street, straight on up through Waterford Street and out onto Marlborough Street. And there it was, the Pro Cathedral, the scene of my baptism all those years ago and where my Auntie Polly stood for me, she was my Godmother. The priest was downstairs in the little chapel sorting himself out. He turned around when he heard our footsteps, we almost went in on our tippy toes.

My mother genuflected and blessed herself in front of him. I just stood there with my hands in my pockets because I didn't know what else to do. *"Excuse us Father..."* said my mother in a whispered voice, *"...this is my Young Fella I was telling you about"*. The Priest looked me up and down and so I looked him up and down in return, only a bit more slowly. He never addressed my mother or asked her my name, he just stood there with a scowl on his face. And I still had no idea what this was all about.

The Priest raised his voice quite a bit and it almost seemed as if the little chapel had been hit by an earthquake. I jumped with fright at the sound of his bellowing voice. *"Can you read and write"?* he asked me. *"Yes Father, I can do both"*, I replied straightaway. I don't think he was too pleased with my answer.

He then handed me a small Prayer Book and told me to read out the first paragraph. I took the book in my hands and looking down at the pages, I became more confused than ever, I had no idea what I was looking at. *"Ah I see..."* said the Priest with a great big grin cutting across his face. *"...I thought you said you could read..."* *"I can Father..."* I said *"...but I don't know what this says"*. *"...that my boy, is God's own language, that's the Latin words of the Mass and if you can't read that then you'll never become a Priest"* he said with a look of joy on his smug face.

I was even more confused now than I was when my mother

told me to get up and wash my face. *"But I don't want to be a Priest, Father"* I blurted out and that's when my mother came in on the conversation. *"Ah but he really does Father, he just doesn't know it yet".*

So, that was the game, my mother wanted me to become a priest, she had another thing coming if I had any say in it. *"You see Father…"* she said, *"…I don't want him ending up in Artane like all his pals and I thought maybe he could study for the priesthood instead, you know what I mean Father".* *"Right so…"* he said to my mother *"…leave it with me and I'll see what I can do in the meantime".* My mother genuflected and blessed herself once again and placed a Half Crown into his hand. *"God bless you Father,"* said my mother. He never said a word, we were just dismissed.

As we walked out of the chapel, I caught a look of him from the corner of my eye, he was staring down at the money my mother had given him and then shoved it into his pocket. I was fuming at his arrogant attitude and I suppose more so because he had caught me out with his Latin Mass Book. And that Half Crown was a small fortune to my poor mother, she could feed us for a couple of days with that.

I had only a short time to go before I finished my schooling in Rutland Street and I wasn't sorry to be leaving either.

155

Somehow, I always managed to keep my head down and was rarely in trouble with any of my teachers. I could never see any sense in skipping off school or *"Mitching"* as we used to call it, because I knew from some of my pals that all they did when they were on the mitch was to hang around Moore Street waiting for a chance to rob a bit of fruit off of a Dealers stall.

Sometimes they'd go down by the Docks and spend their time there. But they were always looking over their shoulder in case a Policeman came along and nabbed them, that's how most of them ended up in Artane or off down the country in Daingean for four or five years. I had heard enough horror stories from some of these boys who had already spent time in these Industrial Schools and I was determined that I wasn't going to end up in one.

Thankfully, my mother never heard anything further from the priest in the Pro Cathedral. It was soon afterwards that one of my pals tipped me off about a job on a Messenger Bike, delivering meat for a butcher. I remember going into the shop for an interview with the head butcher.

He had a fine big belly on him and a great big knife in a wooden case hanging by his side. *"Well, young man..."* he said, in a friendly kind of voice, *"...and how well do you know your way around Dublin"*. I stuttered and stammered a bit and then replied *"Oh yeah, I know everywhere, honest I do"*. And so, I got the job, I began my working life in Dodrill's Butchers' Shop in Moore Street.

Now, what I didn't realise at that time was, and nobody ever told me either, Dublin didn't only extend from East Wall to Capel Street and up as far as Dorset Street, most every place on the south side of the River Liffey was also Dublin. It was my father who told me that. My mother said I'd never get lost as long as I had a mouth and could ask people the way, and that's exactly what I did. Deliveries became easier as time went on because I nearly always went to the same customers every time and I rarely got lost anymore.

I really enjoyed my time working as a Messenger Boy. Some Saturday's I used to get a lump of meat to bring home to my mother and it was free of charge. I remember cycling up O'Connell Street one day with several deliveries and whistling my head off and without a worry in the world when all of a sudden, I tried to turn the handlebars on my bike because I was going around the corner into Parnell Street and that's when it happened.

What with my carefree attitude and my man-of-the-world

face on me, I failed to notice that the front wheel of my bike was stuck in the groove of the tram track and it refused to turn for me. Up I went, head over heels and landed down on the bundles of meat that I was carrying. The butcher had the meat all neatly wrapped up in bundles and the names and addresses of each customer written on them but not now they weren't, they had all burst open when I landed on them and everything was mixed up. The basket off my bike was over the other side of the road near the Ambassador Picture House. So, back to the shop I had to go. The lads in the shop all burst out laughing when they heard what had happened. The butcher told me to pay them no attention because it could easily happen to a Bishop.

As time went on, I was allowed to work in the shop alongside the older lads. They would show me how to cut the meat and tell me the names of all the different parts of the animals. I didn't really like working in the small slaughterhouse out at the back of the shop. Although I never saw the animals being killed, I could hear them bellowing and squealing out in a very frightened manner.

My job was to clean up the place after the animals had been slaughtered. I remember the first time I was allowed to serve a customer. This woman came in and asked me for an

Ox Tail. I was stumped, because the lads had never mentioned that thing to me and I had no clue as to what it was. So, me being me, I went out to the back of the shop and brought in a cow's tail. After that fiasco I was confined to selling sausages and pudding only. But eventually I got the knack of things and began working full-time behind the counter.

It was around this time that Dublin Corporation offered my father and mother a new Flat further down the street near Beaver Street, the Flats were called Liberty House. Well, the poor oul Ma' was so excited, she thought all her Christmases had come in one parcel. And sure, wasn't Polly and Fingers offered one as well. That was such a great time for us all.

No more having to go down all them stairs and out to the back yard for a bucket of water. My father could stand out on the balcony and smoke his fags while he watched the world go by. We were posh now, with proper electricity and we even had a bath and a Gas Stove that my mother could do all her cooking on, no more having to stoke up the fire to boil a kettle of water for her cup of tea. Moving in to a proper Flat gave a great boost to us all.

Most of what we had in the way of furniture in our old tenement room was left behind, it had all seen better days and was only fit for the dump. With the extra money coming in from myself, Jimmy, Tommy and Vera, we managed to get some really good quality second-hand furniture. My father made sure to take down the Sacred Heart picture that was always hung up over our mantlepiece in the old Flat, that was a wedding present they were given by his own mother. I remember my mother was in tears because she was moving away from all her old neighbours. My father got a great laugh out of telling her that they too were moving into the Flats next to us.

At one time there were ten families living in our tenement house and then there was Mister O'Reilly who lived in the basement, he used to walk with a limp because during the War a German soldier shot him in the leg and he was never right since. He used to always get me to run to the shops for his Woodbine cigarettes, my father used to call them *"Coffin Nails"*.

The whole area where I grew up and spent my younger years was to be demolished, all the little side streets would be gone, no more Elliott Place or Faithful Place and even Purdon Street was to be demolished. The old schoolhouse my father went to was coming down as well and Joe O'Reilly's pub on the corner of Railway Street and Elliott

Place was due to get the hammer, that's where my father used to drink, mainly because old Joe would serve him up a free pint now and then. And so, the playground of my childhood would be no more.

Times were certainly changing alright, we were all grown up and my parents, as well as my Auntie Polly and Fingers too, were beginning to show their age. Around this time, I had dated a few different girls alright but nothing more serious than a night at the Pictures. The one that I dated for the longest time, about six weeks, was Dolores Hadden, she worked on the Cash Register in the butcher shop where I worked.

She lived with her parents and a few brothers in a small house down off the North Strand. Her father wasn't too keen on me since he heard that I was from the Flats in Railway Street and her mother was ever so posh, she didn't eat meat of a Friday and wasn't too keen on me being a butcher in case I'd encourage her daughter to do so.

Most of the lads I went to school with had taken the boat to England in search of work. Others just hung around the street corners and the Bookie Shops, an odd one or two worked part-time down the Docks. Most of their marriages had gone stale within two months of the wedding day. It was all this stuff going around in my head that got me thinking about my own future. What direction was I heading?

I remember when my father went to the Dispensary on Summerhill to see the Doctor, he said he was finding it hard to breath. Then off he was sent to the Mater Hospital for tests and the results weren't good, my father was diagnosed with cancer of the throat. We were all in shock at this news, what where we expected to say to people and what were we expected to do? My mother and my Aunt Polly spent most of their time crying into each other's arms.

My father lay in his hospital bed unable to talk. This was not him at all because he loved talking and would do so for hours at a time. I would sit beside him holding his hand and singing in a low voice, his favourite song, his party piece my mother used to call it. I knew every word of it so well because it was the only song I had ever heard him singing, it was called *"My Mother's Eyes"*.

A few days later one of the young nurses from the hospital called by the butcher's shop and asked me to bring the family up to the hospital, she told me that my father would only last a matter of hours.

And that's how it was, with my Aunt Polly on one side of the bed holding his hand and my mother doing the same on the other side. When my father ever so slowly closed his eyes and slipped away into eternity, Fingers began reciting a decade of the Rosary and we all answered in hushed tones, with tears freely streaming down our cheeks. There are really no words to describe how I felt at that very moment or how any of us felt.

On the day of his funeral my mother was dressed from head to toe in black and that's how she remained for the rest of her life, forever in mourning. She rarely ever laughed after he died. She would spend most of the time on her knees in the church with her Rosary Beads. She was never the same.

A couple of weeks after the funeral my sister Vera and her boyfriend, Sonny Bellew, announced that they were getting married and had plans to emigrate to Australia. After WWII the British government were looking for young families in particular to emigrate to Australia to help populate that country and had offered an assisted passage for ten pounds sterling. Anyone from Ireland wanting to take up the offer had to be born before 1949.

Vera said that they had made that decision quite some time ago and had planned to sit down with my father and mother and tell them all about it. My mother gave them her blessing and told Vera and Tommy to do what they felt was best for themselves as a couple. She was heartbroken of course but that was always how my mother was, she'd never stand in our way of making something good of ourselves.

The wedding was a quiet affair with family and a few close friends of the newlyweds there. Before any of us knew where we were, Vera and Tommy were gone off on a boat to Australia, six weeks at sea.

Time marched on and I went back to working in the shop, cutting and chopping up meat and always making sure to smile at all of our customers because my brother Jimmy said that's just how it had to be and Tommy said he agreed with him.

They were both working fulltime now, Jimmy was a Waiter in the Gresham Hotel, one of his football pals fixed that up for him. He loved telling us about all the Toffs and famous Hollywood stars who stayed in the hotel and about all the tips he used to get. He had a great collection of autographs of a lot of famous people. The one that he treasured most was Roy Rogers autograph, he was the famous Hollywood Cowboy that we used to see in the Picture House when we were young fellas.

Tommy got himself a job with Tonge and Taggart, the iron

foundry people, he was employed as a Pattern Maker, whatever that was I never really knew but it was a well-paid job. They both had plans of their own in the pipeline for their future, they had applied for work in Canada and had been accepted but it would be some time before everything kicked into place for them to leave home.

I have never forgotten that particular Saturday, the morning had started off in the usual manner. Up out of bed at the last minute, dashing around looking for my shoes, trying to get a cup of tea into myself and just as I was about to charge out the door I stopped, something was different, I felt it inside my gut but what it was I couldn't figure out.

I walked over to the door of my mother's bedroom and quietly opening it, I looked in to check that she was alright. She was still in bed and seemed as though she was fast asleep. I ever so quietly closed the door so I wouldn't disturb her. I headed out to work. That single hesitation bothered me all day long and my mind wasn't really on my work, more than twice I had wrapped up a piece of meat for a customer that they hadn't asked for. *"My mother never slept late"*, I told myself.

Sometime around three o'clock I decided to take a break and make myself a cup of tea. As I walked towards the back of the shop I stopped in my tracks and slowly turned my head. It didn't make sense what I was looking at, what were they doing here?

In the doorway of the shop stood my Aunt Polly and Fingers, she was crying into her hankie and Fingers gave me the nod to go outside, he had something to tell me. Earlier, Polly had called to my mother's Flat because they had made plans the day before to go shopping together for some new Net Curtain material in Guiney's.

My mother always left the hall door key in the door and Polly always let herself in whenever she called, that's just the way it was with them. When she was inside, Polly called out my mother's name several times but got no reply. She decided to check in the bedroom and that's when she found my mother, she had finally gone to join my father. Polly said that my mother never stopped talking about my father and that she most probably died from a broken heart because she missed him so much.

I have no memory of leaving my job after hearing this tragic news. Everything and everyone just became a great big blur. Now I knew why it was that I hesitated that Saturday morning as I was about to leave for work. My mother was buried in with my father, that's what they both would have wanted. Vera never managed to get home from Australia for the funeral. My boss let me ring Australia from the shop and I was then able to talk to her and tell her what had happened. We both cried non-stop over the phone.

It wasn't too long after the funeral that Jimmy and Tommy told me that they were given the all clear for Canada and that they would be leaving within a fortnight.

For quite some time afterwards I didn't know if I was coming or going, there were too many changes happening too quickly. I remember saying goodbye to my two brothers in Dublin Airport, the last I ever saw of them was boarding the plane to Canada and I remember how excited they both were.

I seem to remember it was a Monday afternoon, everything was quiet in the shop and most of the lads had gone home early, when the clanging of the bell over the shop door intruded on my thoughts. Three young ladies came in through the door, full of giggling noises and the three of them chatting away all at the same time. *"Now ladies, what can I get you"* I said with a broad, friendly smile across my face.

The three of them giggled even louder than before. The one with the Beehive Hairstyle said, *"We've never been called ladies before"* and turning to her two friends, they all laughed out as loud. This of course had me laughing too but at what I had no idea. The Beehive stared straight at me and said *"My pal wants you to take her out on a date"*. I laughed of course because I thought this was part of some joke or other. When I didn't answer straightaway the young lady with the fringe said *"Well, is that a yes or a no"?*

I didn't know what the heck was going on here, were they joking me or were they serious and who was I expected to take out on a date anyway? The third member of the party stepped forward and said *"Well, are you going to ask me out or what"*? And that's how it all started.

Six months later I was married to Alice Finnegan, daughter of Jimmy and Noreen from the Croke Park end of the North Circular Road. We had our wedding reception in the North Star Hotel and all of the meat for the meal was supplied free of charge, courtesy of my boss, Mister Dodrill.

We went out to Bray for a fortnights honeymoon, we got fed up out there after three days because it never stopped raining and so we decided to head home to my mother's Flat where we intended to settle down and live out the rest of our days together.

Alice worked in a sewing factory in Mary Street and

stayed on working after we were married. Almost every Saturday night we would meet up with my Aunt Polly and Fingers for a few drinks and a catch-up, sometimes Mister and Misses Finnegan would join us. On our way home we would always buy some fish and chips for our supper.

One Saturday night in particular, Polly and Fingers never showed up. This was most unusual because normally, if they couldn't make it out on any particular night, Polly would always let Alice know beforehand. I think Alice loved Polly just as much as I did. I remember it was a freezing cold night when we arrived at the door of their Flat. I never had to knock on their door because Fingers had given me a key of my own and told me just to let myself in any time I was calling by, and that's what I did. I half expected to hear some sort of noise, the two of them chatting away to each other or music coming out of the wireless, sometimes they used to sit in of an evening listening to Radio Luxemburg.

Their Flat was as quiet as a mouse, not a sound and not even a light on. I was getting that feeling again that I had on the morning my mother died. I held Alice by the hand as I slowly opened the bedroom door and switched on the light. And there they were, Polly and Fingers, lying side by side and not a sign of life in either one of them. I just stood there mesmerized, unable to take a breath, this just couldn't be happening.

Alice put her hand up to her mouth as she let out a high-pitched scream. *"No, no, this can't be happening"*, she cried. I turned out the light and left the two of them where they lay. Alice and I went to find a Priest and to let her parents now what had happened. My Auntie Polly and Fingers had both died in their sleep, in or around the same time as each other. It was the strangest thing ever and no doctor or priest could ever explain to me what had happened. What we wanted to meet up with Polly and Fingers for was to tell them our good news, Alice was expecting a baby, she was three months gone.

I soon realised, as I was helping with the funeral arrangements, that I had no way of contacting my brothers, Jimmy and Tommy, in Canada, as I had heard nothing from them since they left Ireland some years previous. I tried ringing Vera in Australia but without any success.

I tried contacting the International Operator to see if they could get through to her number, *"Sorry sir, but that number is no longer in service"* was the only reply I got. Polly and Fingers were buried in the same plot as my father and mother, they were back once more in each other's company.

I made sure to have their names put on the headstone alongside my parent's names.

Alice and I took on the job of clearing out Polly's Flat because the Corporation wanted to rent it out to a young couple with three little children. Alice said that she knew this couple and suggested that maybe they'd like to keep some of Polly's furniture. And so, they moved in to an almost completely furnished Flat. I soon realised that without Alice, I would have no one in my life.

I was just walking along our balcony this particular morning when our Postman appeared at the top of the stairs, *"Ah..."* he said when he saw me, *"...the very man. Just sign your name here and it's all yours"*. He handed me a registered brown envelope and disappeared back down the stairs. I wasn't too sure what this was about, maybe something from the Tax-Man, so I shoved it in my inside pocket and continued on my way to work.

We were quite busy in the shop that day and what with fresh cattle arriving in for butchering from the Cattle Market in Prussia Street, I never got a minute to myself and my brown envelope. At around four o'clock everything began to slow down and so I slipped out to the back yard and opened up my envelope.

It was from a Solicitor's Office in Dorset Street, I was to call in to the office at my earliest convenience to discuss a matter of legal importance. I rang the number of this office and a very posh speaking secretary answered. I explained about my letter and she said *"That's fine, tomorrow morning at ten o'clock will suit Mister Darnley."* And she hung up.

When I arrived home from work that evening, I couldn't wait for Alice to get home from the sewing factory to tell her about the Solicitor's letter. She read the letter and then looking at me with a worried frown on her face said *"Are we in trouble or what"? "I have no idea love..."* I said to her, *"...we'll just have to wait and see".* The next morning Alice told one of her work pals to tell their boss that she wasn't well and wouldn't be going into work that day. We made our way up along Summerhill and turning onto the North Circular Road, we headed for the *"Big Tree"* pub on the corner of Dorset Street.

According to the directions in the letter, the solicitor's office was a few doors down from the pub. It was situated up over a Newsagent's Shop and we had to ring the doorbell to get in. The Secretary, Miss Fitz, told us that we would have to wait for about ten minutes or so. There was another door in this office with a name displayed on it, *"James E.*

Darnley, Solicitor", that must be him, I thought to myself. The next thing was the door opened and an older woman came out first, crying into her handkerchief, followed by Mister Darnley himself who was trying to give her words of comfort. *"At least you won't be depending on the Social Welfare, Misses Quinn..."* he said to her, *"...your husband made sure to see to that"*. And out she went.

Then it was our turn and Mister Darnley ushered us into the crammed little space he called his office, it had all sorts of books scattered around the place, on the floor, the window ledge and all over his desk. He invited us both to sit down. *"Now..."* he said, *"...there's nothing to worry yourselves about, it's all straight forward enough, all I need is a signature and I can give you the cheque, then you can be on your way"*.

He went on to explain that my Aunt Polly and Fingers had come to see him six months previous. They had made out a small Will and had left me a sum of money, five hundred pounds in total. I looked at Mister Darnley in amazement and blurted out *"Five hundred pounds? Sure, that's a small fortune"*. He looked back at me over the rim of his glasses and smiled.

Alice gave me a nudge to sign my name, which I did and

173

taking Mister Darnley by the hand, I gave it a good shake and thanked him most profusely. I think myself and Alice danced down the stairs and out onto the street like we were Fred Astaire and Ginger Rogers. What in Heavens name were we going to do with five hundred pounds?

Amid giggles and laughing out loud we made our way across the road to the Hibernian Bank in Dorset Street. I asked if we could speak to the Manager. After about fifteen minutes of a wait, he came out and invited us into his office, which was much neater and tidier than the one across the road where Mister Darnley worked.

I showed the Bank Manager the cheque and explained where we got it from but we didn't know what to do with it because neither Alice nor myself had ever been inside a Bank before. The Manager, Mister Dooley, asked me what I worked at and I told him I was now a Master Butcher. He suggested that maybe we could think about buying our own house with the money and that my wages would be a great help as well.

Alice leaned over and whispered in my ear that she was feeling dizzy and getting pains from the baby inside her. I thought it was from all the excitement until I looked at her and knew her time had come. I quickly handed Mister

Dooley the cheque and asked him to mind it for me because we had to get to the Rotunda Hospital straightaway. He called in one of his staff and told the young fella to drive us to the hospital in a hurry.

Well, in next to no time at all I was looking at Alice sitting up in the hospital bed and holding our little baby daughter in her arms, she looked like a little Angel straight from Heaven. Up to this point we had given no thought as to what name we were going to call the baby when it arrived because we had no idea if it was going to be a girl or a boy. Before I could say anything, Alice beat me to it. *"We're going to have her baptised as Pauline but we're going to call her Polly, after your Auntie Polly"* and that settled that.

It wasn't too long after Baby Polly was born and with the help of Mister Dooley in the Bank, that we began to settle in to our new home. We bought a small terraced house just around the corner from the North Strand Picture House, we had no front garden but the one out back was big enough for what we needed. I was cycling in and out to work each day and Alice was doing some Home-Work for the sewing factory. Mister Dodrill had retired from the butcher shop but had convinced me to rent the business from him, in that way I could be my own boss, I was on top of the world.

Two or three days after we celebrated Baby Polly's first birthday Alice went to see our Doctor on the North Strand, she hadn't been in good form lately and thought she might just need a tonic bottle or something to help perk her up. Doctor Mulally checked her out and told Alice that he had some concerns and would arrange for her to attend the Mater Hospital for further tests. When Alice came home and told me this news, I tried to put her mind at ease by saying it was probably nothing and not to be worrying herself over it.

Alice went for her tests and was diagnosed with lung cancer; she was taken into hospital straightaway. This didn't make sense to either one of us because Alice was never a smoker and neither was I. Within two weeks I had lost the love of my life.

My whole world collapsed around me, I was unable to function as I once did, After the funeral, Alice's father and mother took on the responsibility of looking after Baby Polly, I just wasn't able to cope. I ended up in Grangegorman hospital with a nervous breakdown. I had lost all track of time and space; I didn't know who I was anymore.

My stay in the hospital lasted no more than three months and for most of that time I was lost inside a vacuum of severe medication and wandering about in a dream-like existence. I actually remember very little of what could be described as normality. Then the day finally came when I was told I could go home.

One of my pals from the butcher shop collected me in his car. I remember he was holding me by the elbow and guiding to the car, opening the door for me and helping me into the passenger seat, but why? I was quite capable of doing these things for myself and he kept on asking me if I was alright. *"Of course, I was alight..."* I kept telling myself, *"...otherwise I'd still be in the hospital"*.

The doctor had told me that it would take a few days for me to adjust to being on the outside again. After my friend dropped me off at my house I sat in there alone, not sure what to do next, so I went to bed.

The next morning, I made my way to my In-Laws on the North Circular Road, I wanted to see Baby Polly. I walked to their house rather than take the bicycle, I was a little unsteady on my feet for a while because of the effects of my medication. I eventually arrived at their house and we sat over a cup of tea in silence, I didn't know what to say and they were very much the same. They were still in mourning for Alice just as much as I was.

On my way home I walked all over town, looking for familiar places, looking for my past but it was gone. I walked along Railway Street looking for my childhood years but there was nothing there. I eventually arrived home. A few days later I decided to return to work, I had to do something to occupy my thoughts and I felt that this was the best option I had. Eventually and gradually, I seemed to find some kind of semblance of what was once for me normality.

It was agreed that Baby Polly would remain with her grandparents for the foreseeable future and that I would see her every Sunday after Mass. We would spend time together in the park in Mountjoy Square, she looked so like Alice that it hurt. Slowly but surely, I was beginning to regain something of what I once was, I was smiling a lot more than usual, business in the shop was doing really well and most evenings I would cycle out to Dollymount Strand for a walk.

It was while I was standing out by the Holy Mary statue in Dollymount, watching a ship passing by the lighthouse in Ringsend on its way to England, that some kind of thought came into my head. It was some months later that I began making plans to leave Ireland and move to England, on my own. I reckoned that Baby Polly was better off with her grandparents. I couldn't go trapezing around England looking for work with her in tow, it just wouldn't be fair to her. I spoke to Alice's parents about my proposed plan, they weren't too happy with it but they eventually agreed it was probably for the best.

After sometime, I sold my house and gave half of the money to Alice's parents, they refused to take it at first but I insisted, they were now coming up to retirement age and would need a bit more income to help raise young Polly. I didn't have farewell drinks with my pals from the shop, we just shook hands and wished each other well for the future. Mister Dodrill had given me the name and address of a cousin of his who ran a number of butcher's shops in Liverpool. He said that he had already contacted his cousin and told him to expect me any day soon.

His cousin's wife ran a boarding house where I could stay until I got on my feet. And everything was almost as simple as that. I said a short goodbye to Baby Polly and Jimmy and Noreen and told them that I'd be in touch as soon as I settled into my new job. Noreen handed me a small photograph of Alice, taken on the day that she made her First Holy Communion, it was like looking at baby Polly. I carefully placed the photograph inside my wallet and said goodbye.

The next day I cycled out to Glasnevin to visit my parents

grave and I told them and my Auntie Polly and Fingers of course, what my plan was and said I hoped they didn't mind too much. I stood all alone over the grave of my beloved Alice, I hoped she'd understand what I was doing and why I was doing it. I kissed her headstone and walked away.

Early the following morning I caught a train from Connolly Station out to Dunlaoghaire. As the train trundled along through the suburbs of the southside of the city I started picking out streets that had become familiar to me when I was delivering meat to houses there on my Messenger Bike.

I could even remember the names of some of the customers, Misses O'Leary with the poodle dog, Miss McCabe the piano teacher, Mister Burke, a retired school teacher and Mister McCarthy who was a retired detective from the Garda Siochana. He was originally from County Cork and he used to tell me great stories about chasing gangsters all around Dublin.

I couldn't believe that I could remember them so clearly after all these years. I wondered for a moment if they remembered me as clearly as I remembered them. The train picked up speed as it cleared the suburbs, heading out along the coast and finally reaching its destination.

The mail boat was crammed with passengers, young families with lots of children, a group of Nuns dressed in blue and a group of country lads, each carrying a small brown suitcase tied tight with a neck-tie or two and a leather belt just in case. There were many other people, like myself, on their own.

The journey over was pleasant enough, three hours of sitting out on the deck in the fresh sea air did me a world of good. One elderly woman that sat beside me began to engage me in conversation. She told me that she had several rings of Black and White pudding in her suitcase, she had used some of her husband's socks to put them in so as to fool the Customs man.

On our arrival in Holyhead we disembarked, there was no problem with the Customs or the Black and White Pudding. And so, I boarded a train for Liverpool. I sat in a carriage on my own. I had to make a change of trains in Chester and that was the only break in this journey that I had to make.

I eventually walked out of Liverpool's Lime Street train station with my suitcase in one hand and a piece of paper with an address on it in the other. I looked around at my new strange surrounding trying to make sense of where I was.

"Are you looking for some place in particular sir" a very Liverpool voice called out. I turned around and found myself facing an English Bobby, an actual Policeman, with one of them big tall hats on his head, he looked like he had just stepped down off the screen in the North Strand Picture House back in Dublin.

He grinned at the surprise look on my face. *"It's alright sir, we don't bite, well not the first time anyway"* he said with a grin. I explained that I had just arrived over from Dublin and showed him my piece of paper with the address I was to go to. As it happened, his grandparents were from Ireland, a small village in County Galway. He told me the address I was looking for was in a place called Wavertree, a short enough distance outside town, by taxi. He walked me over to the nearby taxi rank and had a word with the first driver in the line of parked taxis. He wished me well and sent me on my way.

I soon arrived at my destination and was met at the door by Mister Dodrill's cousin and his wife, Ernie and Olive Bradshaw. They were a typical English couple, very pleasant and likable. Olive showed me up to my room and told me to be sure to make myself at home. Downstairs, Ernie already had the tea ready for us. I could see that Olive had taken out her good China for my arrival.

I remembered when we lived in the tenement room, my mother used to give us our tea in a Jam Jar and that's the way it was until we moved into Liberty House, then we got proper cups and saucers. Olive said that their daughter, Beryl lived with them as well and I'd hopefully meet her later on that evening. Ernie told me that I could start work the following morning in the shop where he himself worked and it was just around the corner and down the road a piece, that's the way he said it.

Ernie took me out for a walk around the neighbourhood *"Just so you'll know your way around"*, he said. He told me that himself and Olive didn't like anyone to smoke in the house or to come in drunk. He was really just filling me in on the basic rules of the house and I appreciated that. He said that his cousin had filled him in a little on my background and said that I came highly recommend as a butcher. He said *"Now Eddie, your business is your business and I won't ask you anything about it but if you ever need someone to talk to, then I'm your man"*. We became the best of friends there and then and remained so for many more years to come.

I soon settled in to a regular routine and wrote home to Jimmy and Noreen every Sunday night and always made sure to include a little message for Baby Polly. One day she told her grandparents that she was now six years old and was not to be called Baby Polly any more, just Polly. They sent me some photographs taken of her on the day of her sixth birthday, I could hardly believe she was growing up so quickly and now she was in school as well.

I eventually met Ernie's and Olive's daughter, Beryl, when she came rushing into the dining room one Sunday morning as I was finishing off my breakfast. *"Oh, hello, who are you"?* she asked as she made her way towards the teapot. I stood up and told her my name was Eddie and I was the new lodger. *"Oh, you're that chap from Ireland my Mum was telling me all about, I can tell from your accent".* And then she was gone, back up to her room with a cup of tea in her hand.

Over time I began to see more of Beryl and we'd often sit and chat by the fire in the Livingroom if we had nothing better to do of an evening. I told her all about my daughter Polly and she suggested that I should arrange for her to come over on holiday, she said Polly could sleep in her room with her.

Soon enough, I wrote to Polly and invited her over for a visit. She was now almost eighteen years old and hoping to get a place in University, I was so proud of her. I wondered at the time what would my Aunt Polly and Fingers make of that, imagine one of our family going to university, sure my father would be wondering where Polly got her brains from. And so, it was all arranged, Polly would arrive in Liverpool airport in a couple of weeks time. Or so it was planned, until I got a telephone call from her Granny. Poor oul Grandad Jimmy was taken into hospital after having a massive stroke and things weren't looking too good for him. I spoke to Polly and she was in pieces over her poor grandad. She apologised for having to cancel her holiday. *"Don't be worrying about that at all..."* I told her, *"...sure we'll arrange it another time. You look after your granny and be sure to let me know how grandad gets on".*

Unfortunately, poor Jimmy didn't last much longer. As I was making arrangements to fly over to Dublin for his funeral Beryl said that she would like to go with me. *"I asked my mother if it would be alright..."* she said, *"...and she said she'd have to check it with my father and so, they gave me the okay to go, if you want me to that is".* It was fine by me of course but I wasn't sure why she wanted to come with me, she'd never been to Ireland before.

I made all the travel arrangements for myself and Beryl. I

booked us into two rooms of a B&B a couple of doors up from the Labour Exchange in Gardiner Street. We'd stay for three days and head back to Liverpool, that was the original plan anyway.

After the funeral in Glasnevin, I brought Polly and Beryl to see my parents grave and I showed them my Aunt Polly's and Fingers details as well. I then took them over to see where Alice was buried. Beryl had bought a small bunch of flowers from the Flower Seller outside the gate of the graveyard, I don't remember seeing her buying them. She handed them to Polly and suggested she place them on Alice's grave.

There weren't many at Jimmy's funeral, a cousin of his that he'd never mentioned before and a few old neighbours. And then there was Eileen, she was a sister of Granny Noreen's. We ended up in the Addison Lodge for something to eat, the cousin and the neighbours all went home. We sat ourselves down and ordered some drinks so that we could raise a glass to wish Jimmy well on his journey up to Heaven.

Beryl was sitting over beside Polly, Eileen and Noreen. I was standing by the window looking over at the gates of the Botanic Gardens, a place I was never in and all the years I spent growing up in Dublin. When I was a Young Fella, there were certain places that I always felt I wasn't allowed into because I wasn't educated enough or I came from the wrong side of the tracks, so to speak. The Botanic gardens would have been one of them places, the grounds of Trinity College were another and the same with the Art Gallery and the Museum in Kildare Street. I also felt that Christchurch Cathedral and Saint Patrick's Cathedral were also out of bounds because I wasn't a Protestant.

I was brought out of this school of thought by Beryl calling over to me. I went and sat beside the girls, now I knew by the looks on those faces that something had been planned behind my back. It was Noreen who broke the ice. *"Eddie..."* she said, *"...we were just saying, why don't you bring Polly back with you to Liverpool when you and Beryl are going"?* Now, there's a way to ask a man a question and sure wasn't the decision already made, what could I say?

And so it was that Noreen and Eileen came out to see us off at the airport, I made sure to give the two of them a great big hug. I was so excited at having Polly travelling with us. We had our three seats together on the plane with Polly seated in by the window so that she could look out at the scenes below. As we were flying out over the Irish Sea Polly turned away from the window and looking across Beryl at me, she said *"Dad, when are you and Beryl going to get married"*?

Well, I can tell you here and now, I wasn't expecting that one. For a split second I wondered if this too was planned back in the Addison Lodge, Beryl just sat there with a great big grin on her face. Before we had landed in Liverpool Beryl had asked Polly to be her Bridesmaid and on and on, they went. I wasn't quite out of the taxi at Ernie's house when he came out and started shaking me by the hand. *"Welcome into the family..."* he said with a great big grin, *"...it took you long enough"*. The next thing I know Olive has me in a strangle hold of a hug and the tears streaming down her face. *"My little girl is going to get married"*, she was saying, in between the tears.

Polly was on the phone later that night telling Noreen all about her flight and the good news that her Daddy was going to marry Beryl. Two days later Ernie told me that he had squared everything up with the local priest, we'd be married before Polly headed back to Dublin. Everything was happening so quick that my head was in a constant spin. And that's how it went.

Ernie had arranged to have the Flat up over his butcher's

shop in the High Street redecorated and fitted out for us to move into. *"I don't want a pair of honeymooners living under my roof"* he laughed. Polly and Beryl were more like sisters than stepmother and stepdaughter. From the moment that Polly arrived back in Dublin she was forever on the telephone to Beryl, the two of them talking non-stop for hours on end.

For a wedding present, Ernie had made me a partner in his butchering business and he insisted that I should take the lead role as overall manager. I spoke to him about setting ourselves up as a wholesale outlet for butcher shops in and around the Liverpool area. It was during this period that my mind went back to the day I discovered that my mother wanted me to be a priest, I wondered what that oul priest would think of me now, a successful businessman in Liverpool. It was all thanks of course to Ernie and Olive; I dread to think how I might have ended up without them in my life.

The years rolled on, Polly had finally graduated from university and had landed herself a great job in Guinness's Brewery. Beryl and I were so proud of her achievements. She phoned Beryl one evening and told her that Granny Noreen was very ill in hospital, things weren't looking too good. As soon as we heard back a fortnight later of Noreen's death, we made arrangements to fly over for her funeral.

It wasn't too long afterwards that Polly phoned and asked to speak to me, she spoke in a very unusual low voice. *"Dad..."* she said, *"...I've been speaking with Beryl a lot since my Nanny's funeral and I want to ask you something"*. I certainly didn't want to hear any more bad news; I had no choice but to listen. *"Can I go over to Liverpool and live with you and Beryl..."*? This was certainly a bolt out of the blue. *"...Nanny and Grandad have left me their house and I don't want to live here on my own, I want to sell it because I really want to live with you and Beryl"*.

Ernie told me to make sure that Polly had a job with the wholesale business if she wanted one, give her an office to herself, he insisted. Olive suggested that Polly should live with them and take over Beryl's old bedroom. I could hardly believe how things were working out for us all. Imagine Polly with a bedroom all to herself, a bedroom that was much bigger than the room my Auntie Polly and Fingers had lived in in Elliott Place.

Sure, what would my sister Vera think of that and all the years she had to sleep on the straw bed on our tenement floor. I wondered why it was that I hadn't heard from Vera in such a long time. And so, in next to no time at all, Polly was well and truly tucked up into her new family.

The years rolled on of course, poor old Ernie had passed away to be shortly followed by our beloved Olive. They were both buried side by side in Allerton Cemetery in Merseyside. These were hard times for poor Beryl, thankfully she had Polly to help prop her up when the going got rough.

The butcher trade was going great and I was so glad to have Polly running the accounts department. By this time, she knew the trade almost as good as I did and she had a great working relationship with all of our customers. She made sure to visit each of them once every three months. During the first year of Ernie and Olive leaving us Beryl and I paid a visit over to their grave in Allerton every Sunday after Mass. They had left a Will and stated that Polly was to inherit their house and all of its furnishings and a little money as well. Everything else was left to Beryl and myself, including the business and all of the butcher's shops.

One day I had arranged to meet Polly for a cup of Coffee, there was something I wanted to talk to her about. As we sat in a little café, I told Polly about not hearing anything from my youngster sister Vera in several years and of having no contact with my two brothers from Canada either.

It was some months later, Beryl and I were still living up over the shop, when Polly called to pay us a visit. She told me that she had been in touch with the Australian Embassy in London and had asked for their help in trying to trace my sister Vera. Polly then handed me a piece of paper with Vera's phone number on it.

I don't know what happened me but I burst out in tears and threw my arms around her. I was shaking so much that I had to ask Polly to make the call to Australia for me. The three of us sat in silent expectation at not knowing what was to follow.

A young woman's Australian voice came on the phone. *"Hello this is the Bellew residence, how may I help you"*, we could hear a lot of laughing and giggling in the background because Polly had the phone on speaker. Polly answered, *"I'm ringing from Liverpool, England and I'd like to speak with Vera Bellew who used to be Vera Carroll, please"*. There was total silence from the phone. Then a voice on the other end shouted out, *"Mam, quick, it's for you and they know your name from before you were married to Dad"*. We could hear noises and shuffling in the background and then a voice I still recognised after all these years spoke.

"Hello, who is this"? Polly handed me the phone and I hesitated so as to draw a big deep breath. *"Hello Vera, this is Eddie, your big brother"*. Silence, then a scream, *"Oh my God, oh my God"* is all Vera could manage to say.

I waited for her to calm down and to explain to the people in the background who I was. And the conversation took off from there. Her husband, Sonny Bellew, she told us, had died some years ago. She had a grown-up family of three boys and two girls and the eldest boy was named after me, the other two boys were named after Jimmy and Tommy in Canada, both of whom had died in their early years over there.

Vera wanted to speak to Polly and Beryl, and her girls wanted to speak to their new cousin, there was great excitement all round. And of course, as our conversation came to a close, we promised to keep in touch on a more regular basis and we did.

I had recently reached my sixty fifth birthday and decided to call it a day with the business and retire. Beryl agreed that we should sign everything to do with the business over to Polly, she would become the new boss. When everything was signed, sealed and delivered, Beryl asked me what I had planned on doing next. I told her that I would like to make one more last and final trip over to Dublin, on my own and that I would take the boat over instead of flying.

Polly took over all the arranging for me and booked me into the Gresham Hotel in O'Connell Street for a week. She had planned on putting all the travel expenses through the Company books. She said it was the least the Company owed me. I didn't argue, after all she was now the boss.

I caught the early boat from Holyhead and after a smooth enough journey over I finally landed on Irish soil. Shortly beforehand however, I was standing out on the ships deck when way off in the distance, I spotted the tips of the two great big chimneys near Poolbeg Lighthouse. I felt a surge of excitement at the thought of returning home for one last and final time. On the bus journey into the city, I began remembering once again the names of the people whose meat I had delivered on my Messenger Bike all those years ago, they must all be dead and gone by now.

I walked from the Bus Station in Amiens Street up to the Gresham Hotel and wallowed in the ever-familiar voices of the Dublin people. I passed by Guiney's in Talbot and it seemed as if nothing had changed in that shop since I first left Dublin. I was half expecting my mother and my Auntie Polly to come out holding up net curtain material.

As I came near to the hotel a young voice called out, *"Here Mister, duz you wantta buy a Herald or Press"*? I looked around and saw this boy of no more than maybe twelve years old with a bundle of newspapers under his arm. I bought a copy of the Evening Herald from him and told him to keep the change. *"Ah Jaysus, thank's mister, are you a millionaire"*? I gave him a wink and walked into the lobby of the hotel, if only he knew, I thought to myself.

For each day of my stay in Dublin I headed off in a different direction when I exited the hotel. My first port of call was Glasnevin Cemetery to talk to Alice and to say a final goodbye to my parents and my Auntie Polly and Fingers. I also made sure to visit the grave of Jimmy and Noreen Finnegan, grandparents to my Polly. The Hibernian Bank in Dorset Street was gone as was the solicitor's office across the road.

Mister Dodrill's butcher shop was gone out of Moore Street altogether, it was now a Café and there weren't as many Dealers' selling fruit and fish as there used to be when I was a young fella. Most of the Picture Houses were gone and there was nothing left of my old neighbourhood. The only thing I recognised in Railway Street was the white cross up over the back gate of the Magdalene Laundry. White's

Lane was long gone of course.

I walked in through the Flats of Liberty House and recognised nobody. I would love to have walked down Elliott Place and looked in the window of my Auntie Polly's old room and spend some time talking with Misses Doyle about when she had the back wall knocked down. But it was never to be.

I suppose in some way or other I was glad to be finally heading back to Liverpool and my real home. I couldn't wait to see Beryl and Polly again and to tell them of the places I went to see and how everywhere was so changed since I was a little boy. I even brought them back a present each, a set of table napkins for Beryl that I bought in Clerys, they had *"A present from Dublin"* stitched on them. And for Polly, I bought a gold chain and locket for around her neck so that she can put a photograph of Alice and herself in it.

I stood at the back of the ship and said a sad and fond farewell to the Poolbeg Lighthouse which always reminded me so much of the last time my father brought me out to Dollymount Strand on the crossbar of his bike.

Katie

I will always remember the fright I got from the banging on the door of our room and the roars and shouts of the soldiers that had come for my father. I think he always knew that this hour would come and that's why he insisted on us living in the back-parlour on the ground floor. It was the middle of the night and by the time I was fully awake and sitting up he was halfway out of the window, with my mother throwing his coat out after him. *"Run Tommy..."* she shouted out to him, *"...run for God's sake"*. In no time, he was over the back wall and running up through the hallway of the tenement house at the back of us, with his boots in one hand and his coat in the other. The banging and the shouting increased in volume from the soldiers outside in our hallway. *"Will yis ever wait, for God's sake, I'm comin'..."* shouted my mother, *"...I have to make meself decent"*.

As the door was pushed in, my three younger siblings, Chrissie, Maggie and Billy started crying out with fright. Chrissie slept in beside me on the floor over in the far corner, and the other two, the twins, slept at the foot of my father's and mother's bed. While my mother was trying to delay the soldiers, I jumped up and closed the window my father had escaped through, in the hope that nobody would notice. One of the soldiers, with a great big black moustache sticking out from under his nose, shouted into my mother's face, *"Alright then, where's he hiding"*.

There was nowhere for anyone to hide in our room, I wanted to tell him, all we had was a bed, a sack full of straw, a Sideboard and a small table with two tea chests to sit on and the fireplace. My mother shouted back at the soldiers as they pulled the bed out from the wall to see if my father was hiding under it, *"Who are yis lookin' for"*. *"Your husband, that's who"* replied one of the soldiers in his thick English accent. *"Well, I hope youse find him because that bastard owes me money for our rent..."*, my mother shouted, *"...we'll be evicted out of here next week if I've no money for the rent man, so yis better keep lookin"*. A young soldier spoke to his commanding officer with the moustache, *"Nothing here sir, all clear"*. *"Alright men, let's go, back to the Barracks"*. And out they went.

My mother closed the door after them and sat down on one of the tea chests. She looked across the room at me as I stood by the window, *"Katie..."* she said in a low voice, *"...poke that fire and boil the kettle for me, I think I need a cuppa tea"*. I first off settled the twins back to sleep and put my coat on over my nightdress because I was cold, Chrissie already had her head back down on the straw bed and was sleeping. I threw a few small sticks on the fire and gave it a poking to bring it back to life. It was then I noticed a quiet kind of a knock on our door. My poor worn out mother looked up at me and said *"See who that is Katie"*.

On opening the door, our neighbour, Misses Marshall put her head in, *"Are youse alright Maureen"?* she asked as her eyes searched around the darkened room for my mother. *"Ah come in, Misses M..."* replied my mother, *"...come in and sit down"*. Misses M stepped in, closed the door behind her and sat herself down. They were both sitting there in the silent darkness of our room. I reached up on my tippy-toes and searching around with my fingers, I took a small piece of candle down from off the mantle-piece. I then lit it from the flaming sticks in our fire and walking over, left it on the table. It instantly lit up my mother's tired and worn-out face and Misses Marshall's too. I stood for a moment to look at the eerie dancing shadows the flickering light threw up along the wall above their heads.

I brought the tea pot over to the table and poured the tea out. Misses Marshall was given her tea in the only good tea cup that we had, because she was considered a visitor and my mother was given hers in a medium sized Jam Jar, the bigger Jam Jar was for my father. The two women sat in silence, sipping their tea and lost in thought. I stood over by the window as the rain came down, dribbling and running across the glass panes.

Like my mother and Misses Marshall, I too was wondering about my father, where was he right now? He had probably headed up through the Gloucester Diamond and made his way up the twenty-seven steps to Summerhill, that's where his older brother, my Uncle Francie lived, he'd be grand once he reached there. It was on the day of Francie's funeral, many years later, that I was told he was the key-man in the area that people would go to if they wanted to skip out of the country in a hurry. He had worked as a Foreman down on the Docks and had everyone in his pocket when it came to doing favours.

My mother called over to me, *"Katie, you should get back into your bed, it's too cold to be standing over there by that window"*. I loved having Chrissie in the straw bed with me because she was always boiling hot when she was asleep. I could cuddle into her and the heat would send me off to sleep too. As I lay beside Chrissie, quietly and slowly falling to sleep, my mother started talking to Misses Marshall, *"I honestly don't know what's going to become of us at all Misses M..."* she said, *"...I honestly don't"*. I suppose Misses Marshall was my mother's best pal, she always helped us out whenever she could.

She had seven children of her own, five girls and two boys. Her husband Jimmy, was always away at sea on some boat or other and only came home when the tide was in. He was very good to her though because he had arranged with the shipping company that he worked for, to make a payment out of his wages to his wife every Friday, through the

General Post Office in O'Connell Street. In doing this, he ensured that his family never went hungry.

Whenever Misses Marshall thought things weren't going too well for us, she would always send a few shillings in to my mother. My mother never had to ask mind you; the money would just arrive with no expectation of it ever being paid back.

The next day was a Saturday and I was helping my mother to clean and tidy our room, we did this every Saturday. My mother always liked to have the room looking right in case we ever had any visitors call by after Mass on Sunday. She had two older sisters, Mary Anne and Maggie, they usually called around after eleven o'clock Mass. Neither one ever married, my father used to call them *'Burke and Hare'*, after the two infamous *'Body Snatchers'* from Scotland. Whenever anyone died in our neighbourhood my mother would bring me with her around to her two sisters to let them know the funeral arrangements because they attended every funeral going, it didn't matter if they knew the deceased or not.

My father used to say they only went to funerals in the hope of getting a free drink. They both lived together in a Flat up over a Butcher's shop in Parnell Street and their place was always spotless clean. Himself and the two sisters didn't exactly see eye to eye on many things, if anything at all.

The twins were sitting on the end of the bed being entertained by Chrissie and her doll. I was down on my hands and knees cleaning out the fireplace and my mother was over by the open window, throwing out a basin of dirty water, when suddenly we heard a gentle tap on our door.

I knew it wasn't Misses Marshall's knock. Straightaway I looked across the room at my mother and as she looked back, she raised a finger to her lips, signalling for me to keep quiet. Chrissie put the twins lying down on their pillow and looked across the room at the door. The rap came once more, followed by a man's whispered voice. *"Misses Lawlor, it's Brendan Fagan, Tommy's friend",* said the voice. My mother ever so quietly walked across the room to the door and opened it just slightly. She peered out to see two men standing there, straightaway she recognised Brendan Fagan from the time he brought around a sack of turf to her the time my father was doing a three month stretch in Mountjoy Jail for something or other.

My mother opened the door and invited the two men in. I picked up the twins in my arms and brought them and

Chrissie down the hall to Misses Marshall, I told her my mother had two visitors. She took the three young ones in and told me to go back in to my mother.

When I returned to our room the two men were seated on the tea chests and my mother was sitting on the edge of her bed. I closed the door behind me and sat down beside my mother. Brendan Fagan was the first to speak. *"We heard about the raid first thing this morning and we've spoken to Tommy. He asked us to let you know that he's safe and that he may have to go away for a while until things quieten down a bit. It might be for a couple of months or so"*. *"Well..."* said my mother, *"...I'm glad to hear he's safe. But what about me and the children, what are we supposed to live on while my husbands on the run doing his bit for Mother Ireland? It would have served him better if he had put his family first and not bloody Ireland"*

The two men looked across at each other. It was then that the second man spoke out, *"You need have no worries about that Misses Lawlor, we'll make sure you're looked after. You have our word on that"*. *"Grand so..."* said my mother *"...as long as the children don't go hungry and I have me rent money"*. The two men then excused themselves and left. My mother had a look of relief on her face regarding my father and the fact that we'd have the rent money coming in.

I was almost twelve years old and still in school. We lived in a two-storey house in White's Lane off Railway Street, there were three other families living in the house with us. Misses Marshall lived in the front room downstairs and we lived in the backroom. Upstairs in the backroom was Mister Byrne with his only son, 23-year-old Paddy, who suffered from Shell-Shock, after a bomb had dropped on the trench he was in while fighting the Germans in France.

Poor Paddy was almost buried alive. He suffered with his nerves ever since. Some nights we could hear him through the ceiling and he roaring and shouting that the Germans were going to kill him. His mother, Misses Byrne had died from Consumption when he was ten years old.

In the front room upstairs lived Misses Kelly and her daughter Eileen whose boyfriend was killed by the Black and Tans while he was delivering bread to a hotel over on the southside. They had planned to get married soon and she never got over his death, she suffered from her nerves as well. She used to have to attend a doctor in the Grangegorman Mental Hospital.

Poor oul Mister Kelly was serving time in Kilmainham

Jail. Someone, and it was never discovered who, had informed on him when they saw him burying two rifles and a box of bullets on some waste ground off Gloucester Street. Several British Soldiers were waiting to ambush him when he went back to retrieve the stuff he had buried. They arrested him and two other men who were seen helping him. My father and my Uncle Francie had gone to the courthouse in Kilmainham to take part in a protest over Mister Kelly's arrest, even though they knew he was guilty.

I remember arriving home from school one day and finding my mother and Misses Marshall sitting by the fire in our room. Chrissie was outside playing with her pals and the twins were asleep in the bed. I walked in and put my schoolbag under the table. My mother called me over to the fire. *"Now, Katie..."* she said, *"...I need you to go on an urgent message with Misses Marshall. I can't go in case the police are watching me."* I turned my head and looked at my mother and said, *"What do you mean, why would the police be watching you"*? *"Because of your father, that's why"*, she said. *"Now, keep your coat on and keep your mouth shut, there's a good girl"*.

Misses Marshall stood up and nodded at me to follow her out into the hallway. Her youngest was asleep in a pram up near the hall door. Misses Marshall pushed the pram out onto the street and I followed, I had no idea where we were going or what I was expected to do. As we walked along the street Misses Marshall broke the silence between us. *"Now, Katie, if anyone asks, you're to say you're my daughter and we're going out to Dollymount for a walk with the baby".*

As we headed out over Annesley Bridge on our way towards Fairview, I stopped and gave a tug on the handle of the pram, bringing it to a halt. *"Now, Misses Marshall..."* I demanded, *"...where are we going and why are we going there and why am I to tell people you're my Mammy, I want to know"*? Misses Marshall looked at me with a grin on her face and said *"Ah Katie, sure you're every bit of your mother when she was your age. We're bringing some guns and stuff out to your father, he's hiding in a house out in Clontarf, that's where we're going".* I stood there in shock, what had my father got to do with guns and why was he always hiding and running away from soldiers?

Misses Marshall went on to tell me that the guns and stuff were hidden in the pram underneath the baby. That had me more puzzled than ever. As we were walking along, I noticed some soldiers further up the street, standing at a barricade beneath the overhead railway bridge in Clontarf. I

207

let out a screech in fright. *"Don't be afraid..."* said Misses Marshall, *"...leave it to me".*

Two armed soldiers came out from behind a sandbag barrier and told us to halt. Misses Marshall put her hand in under the baby's blanket and suddenly the poor child gave out an unmerciful roar all over the street. The two soldiers jumped with fright at the screeching of the baby. *"Ah look at what yis done to the poor child..."* shouted Misses Marshall at the two soldiers, *"...sure he has an awful fear of guns and uniforms".* The two soldiers weren't too sure how to handle this situation and so waved us through the barricade without any search of the pram or ourselves being made. When the baby eventually calmed down, I asked Misses Marshall what had happened to the child. *"Ah sure, I just gave him a little pinch on the leg, that always works",* she said with a smile on her face.

After walking for quite some time, Misses Marshall stopped the pram outside the gate of a large house. She looked at me and said, *"Now, Katie, go up to that hall door and give it a gentle knock, not too loud mind yeah".* I asked her *"Who lives in there, Misses Marshall".* *"Now, never you mind, just do as I tell yea while I pretend to be fixing the babby...",* she said as she gave me a look. *"...and don't bang the gate either".*

I opened the gate and quietly closed it behind me. When I got to the hall door, I had to stand up on my tippy-toes to reach the great big door knocker. I gave it two gentle taps. *"Ah for God's sake, a bit louder than that Katie",* Misses Marshall shouted up the pathway at me. So, I gave it a good hard bang that nearly shook the door off its hinges. When the door opened up, I saw this big tall woman standing there, she was dressed all in black. Without saying a word, she looked past me and beckoned to Misses Marshall. The next thing was we were all in the hallway, pram and all and the door was shut behind us.

The stairway in this house was about three times the size of our stairs at home and the hallway was about six times as long, well that's how it seemed to me anyway. *"Ah Katie, come in... ",* said my father's familiar voice, *"...hello Misses Mac, did you bring the goods with yeah"?* There was my father standing in the doorway of a room down at the end of the hallway. I ran down to him and we threw our arms around each other.

I looked up at him with tears dripping out of my eyes and said, *"Da', why don't you come home, we all miss yeah".* He looked at me through his beautiful blue eyes and answered, *"Someday soon, Katie, someday soon"*. I knew then that he didn't mean he was going to walk back home with myself and Misses Marshall. The woman in black called me into the kitchen and asked me to help her make some tea. As I walked in, I noticed Misses Marshall reaching in under the baby in the pram and taking out several things wrapped up in brown paper. My father took them from her and headed up the stairs with them.

And sure, we were no sooner there when it was time to leave. My father gave me a big hug and a silver shilling to put in my pocket. He told me to give my mother and the others a kiss for him. The woman in black thanked Misses Marshall and off we went. But we didn't walk back the way we came. Misses Marshall said it would be better to take the long way home and then we wouldn't have to see the soldiers again. I was glad of that for the baby's sake and the big bruise he had on his leg from our last encounter with soldiers.

On our walk home curiosity was getting the better of me and so I asked Misses Marshall why my father was living in that big house with the woman in black. I asked her did he not love my Mammy anymore. *"How old are you now Katie"?* Misses Marshall asked me. *"I'll be thirteen on my next birthday"*, I told her. She reckoned there and then that I was now old enough to know what was going on but she swore me to secrecy and I was to say nothing to my mother. She told me that my Daddy was in a secret kind of army and that they wanted to get the English soldiers out of Ireland. She said that if the soldiers caught my father that they might shoot at him and that's why we had to bring the guns and bullets to him, so he could shoot back at them. I asked her why my father and his pals couldn't just walk up to the soldiers and ask them to go back to England. *"If only Katie..."* she said *"...if only"*.

I never saw my father again after that day. He wasn't there for my birthday when I became a teenager and he wasn't there for Christmas either. Even Brendan Fagan and his pal stopped calling to see my mother to give her the rent money. She had to go begging to the Saint Vincent de Paul and ask them to put food on our table.

Misses Marshall and her husband moved away and we never heard from them again either. They bought a house in Ringsend and that was miles away from where we lived and he was still sailing around the world. The Welfare people came knocking on our door one day and took Billy and Maggie away from us. They said my mother couldn't manage and so they were put in an orphanage out in Kingstown. My mother threw out the straw bed that Chrissie and myself always slept on. She took Chrissie in the bed beside her and I slept down at the end.

I remember one day when the Postman came knocking on our door. I was sixteen at that time and working at sewing for a man in Foley Street, there were ten of us working there making Habits for dead people. My sister Chrissie was coming up to her fourteenth birthday and had to give up the last few months of her schooling to look after our mother because she wasn't well.

This day we got a postcard from America, from my father, to say that he was now living there and wouldn't be coming back to Ireland. He said nothing about what we were supposed to do, nothing, he never even mentioned any of us by name. That was the news that broke my mother's poor aching heart, her health went downhill from that day onwards.

The man that she had married all those years ago when she was only sixteen years old and who she always loved, didn't want her or his own children anymore. *"So much for him fighting for Mother Ireland, what about the mother of his children"*, I used to say to myself. I remember times when my mother was lying in bed at night, crying and asking God what had she done that was so wrong to deserve this. *"Sure, didn't I always go to Mass every Sunday, ever since the day I made my First Holy Communion and I always went to Confession as well"*, she'd cry into her pillow. Her two sisters would still call by after Mass every Sunday with their *"We told you so"* faces on them. We never heard from my father after that one postcard. My mother's health became so much worse over the next few months.

I remember going over to the Pro Cathedral and asking Father Reid if he would bring some Holy Communion over to my mother because she was so sick and told him she couldn't make it across to Mass. He asked me what was wrong with my mother and I started crying my eyes out and I told him about the postcard from America. He sent me home and promised to follow me over soon. When Father Reid arrived, he had a doctor with him. Myself and Chrissie had tried to clean our room up as best we could.

The doctor had a look of horror on his face when he saw our room. He walked over to the bed and took one look at my mother. *"She can't possibly stay here…"* he said to the priest, *"…I'll have to arrange an ambulance for her and the quicker the better"*. He looked closely into my mother's

213

eyes and then felt for her pulse. He then turned and looked across the room at me. *"Your mother is very sick, I don't think her heart is right, she needs to go to hospital. I'll have her taken to the Union straightaway"*. The doctor told Father Reid that something would have to be done regarding myself and Chrissie. *"They can't be left living in these conditions or they'll follow their mother"*, he whispered ever so quietly to the priest.

Myself and Chrissie stood side by side holding each other's hand. We were frozen together in a moment of horror, *"Is our Mammy going to die"?* I asked the doctor. He looked across at myself and Chrissie and then looking at the priest, he said *"I'm afraid so"* and out he went.

Now I have to say that Father Reid was a very righteous and Christian man where we were concerned. My mother died three weeks after going into hospital. In those three weeks he arranged for a friend of his to take myself and Chrissie into the hospital every night in a motor car.

I remember the last time I saw my mother; she was lying there in the hospital bed holding her Rosary Beads and telling us that she could see Angels all around her room. Myself and Chrissie would cry all the way home. Father Reid made all the funeral arrangements for my mother and got the Saint Vincent DePaul to pay for it. Her two sisters, Mary Anne and Maggie, were old and frail by then, they went home immediately after the funeral Mass.

My mother was buried in a Pauper's Grave in Glasnevin. There was only myself, Chrissie and Father Reid left standing by her grave. The three of us walked home together, covered in a cloud of sadness. There was still no word from our father in America.

Father Reid arranged for myself and Chrissie to move into a couple of clean rooms up over a shop in Marlborough Street. He even got us a bed each, we couldn't believe it, we could never have imagined having a bed all to ourselves. Because Chrissie was now fourteen years old and having finished in school, Father Reid gave her the job of looking after himself and two other priests, she was delighted.

I was still making the dead peoples Habits, I even got a free one for my mother when she was being laid out, one of the women I worked with even sewed the names of my mother's four children into the Habit. Father Reid made inquiries about the twins, Billy and Maggie and it wasn't good news either. He called up to our Flat one evening and told us that the twins had been given to a Catholic couple from Canada and that's where they were now living. He could find no address or name of the couple they went to. Like my father, we never heard from them again.

It was a couple of years after my mother had passed away that Father Reid met me outside where I worked in Foley Street. I got a shock when I saw him first because I thought he was bringing me bad news. *"Ah now, Katie..."* he said, *"...when do I ever bring you bad news"?* He walked me up to Wynne's Hotel in Abbey Street, he said he wanted to treat me to Tea. I had never been in a hotel in my life. To be honest, I felt out of place, it was almost too posh for me. *"Don't be worrying now..."* said Father Reid, *"...we'll just have tea and a little chat"*.

We sat over in the corner of the room and soon enough we were sipping our tea, out of real cups with real saucers, nothing like the jam Jars we used to have in our room in White's Lane. After a few minutes of drinking our tea Father Reid put his cup down on the saucer. *"Now Katie..."* he said to me *"...I have a newspaper here in my pocket and I think there is something in it you might find interesting, have a look".*

He pushed the tea cups and teapot to one side and opened up his paper across the table. He tapped his finger on one particular part of it. *"Now..."*, he said, *"...have a read of that and tell me what you think"*. I looked at where his finger pointed and read it to myself first and then read it out loud. *"Trainee Nurses required for hospitals in England"*. I looked up with a puzzled face at Father Reid. He sat there smiling.

"What are you getting me to read this for Father"? I asked him. *"Well..."*, he said, *"...I think you should answer that, sure you'd make a great nurse altogether"*. I remember my stomach went into a terrible knot; I don't really remember what I was thinking, I was just staring across the table at him.

He said he would look out for Chrissie and make sure she was well looked after. So, three months later, there I was, standing out on the deck of the B&I boat, making my way over to England and waving goodbye to my work pals, Father Reid and my little sister, Chrissie. My mother's two sisters told me I wouldn't last a week. I couldn't stop crying and laughing at the sadness and excitement of it all, I was going to be a Nurse.

I lost myself in my studies and was determined to be the best Nurse ever. I made some great friends amongst the new recruits I was training with. We used to love flirting with the young trainee Doctors just for the fun of it. After four years of very hard work, I eventually graduated with First Class Honours. My sister Chrissie and Father Reid travelled over from Dublin to be there for me on my *'Big Day'*, my graduation.

In time I became more confident in my nursing and was much later appointed as assistant to the Matron. I wrote to Chrissie almost weekly and now and then to Father Reid. My mother's two sisters passed away within weeks of each other. It was only then that we discovered that they had actually owned the Flat where they lived and the shop underneath as well. I agreed with Father Reid that Chrissie should become the new owner of both. We never heard anything from my Uncle Francie, my father's brother or any of his family since my father went to America, it seems as if they too disowned us.

Neither Chrissie nor I ever married, we used to laugh about that in our letters and phone calls home to each other. We'd mimic my father calling us two oul maids. I was very upset the morning she phoned me with the news of Father Reid's death. Even though she had the Flat and the money from renting out the Shop, she still looked after him, even after he retired. I flew to Dublin for his funeral. It was only then that we discovered that he himself was an orphan or so one of the priests told us at his graveside.

And so, it is as I lay here in my hospital bed that I reminisce about my life. Chrissie is probably in Dublin Airport now, waiting to board her flight on her way over to see me. It seems by all accounts and according to my Medical Team, that I must have inherited my mother's weak heart. I can't wait to see Chrissie; in my head I still call her *'My Little Sister'*.

Other books by this author are available online from

info@choicepublishing.ie

A Time To Remember

Cabra and its People
By
Martin Coffey B.A.

Tell Me A Story

Cabra Remembered

Martin Coffey B.A. (Hons.)

Ambrose O Shea

'*My Neil Diamond Experience*'

Written and compiled by

Martin Coffey B.A (Hons.)

Old Dublin Photos

Paddy Coffey

(1905 – 1989)

Written by

Martin Coffey (B.A. Hons)

**' I always tell the truth
sometimes'**

Written by

Martin Coffey B.A. (Hon's)

MURDER IN THE MONTO

Written and complied

By

Martin Coffey B.A. (Hons)

There's no place like home

Written by
Martin Coffey B.A. (Hons)

The author was also involved in the following publications.

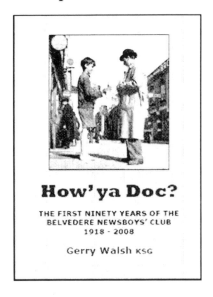

My Renehan Family History

Curraghmore,
County Tipperary

Written and Compiled by
Mary Renehan and Martin Coffey B.A. (Hons)

A PLEIN AIR DIARY

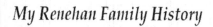

Irene M Dixon